MW01142887

CHUCK FARRIS AND THE LABYRINTH OF DOOM

CHUCK FARRIS AND THE LABYRINTH OF DOOM

Lois Gresh
and
Danny Gresh

ECW PRESS

The publication of *Chuck Farris and the Labyrinth of Doom*
has been generously supported
by the Canada Council, the Ontario Arts Council,
and the Government of Canada through
the Book Publishing Industry Development Program.

CANADIAN CATALOGUING IN PUBLICATION DATA

Gresh, Lois H.
Chuck Farris and the labyrinth of doom

ISBN 1-55022-460-3

I. Gresh, Danny, 1989- II. Title.

PZ7.G864CHU 2001 J813'.54 C2001-9000535-0

Cover design by Guylaine Regimbald – SOLO DESIGN.
Typesetting by Yolande Martel.

Printed by Transcontinental.

Distributed in Canada by General Distribution Services,
325 Humber College Boulevard, Etobicoke, Ontario M9W 7C3.

Distributed in the United States by LPC Group,
1436 West Randolph Street, Chicago, IL 60607, U.S.A.

Distributed in Europe by Turnaround Publisher Services, Unit 3,
Olympia Trading Estate, Coburg Road, Wood Green, London, N2Z 6T2.

Distributed in Australia and New Zealand by Wakefield Press,
17 Rundle Street (Box 2266), Kent Town, South Australia 5071.

Published by ECW PRESS
Suite 200
2120 Queen Street East
Toronto, Ontario M4E 1E2.

ecwpress.com

PRINTED AND BOUND IN CANADA

Dedicated to the memory of Janet Castronova, the founder of Novatek Communications, Inc.

As always, dedicated with great love to Grandpa Sam, who encouraged me to write fiction and who viewed creativity as something worthwhile. And to Rena and Grandma Freda, who continue to put up with me, always with the greatest affection and kindness. Finally, to Dan the Man, the Mountain Man, whose mother has a hundred labyrinths taped to her bedroom wall—it's not easy living with a writer, so I thank you, Dan.

—Lois H. Gresh,
August 2001

Many thanks to our agent, Lori Perkins, and to our publisher, Robert Lecker. Thanks also to Chuck's magnificent publicist, Ellen Libretto.

Tell us what you like about this book! Tell us what you like about the PlayStation2 video games.

On the Internet at

http://www.sff.net/people/lgresh/

and by email: lgresh@rochester.rr.com.

TABLE OF CONTENTS

1

THE DEMON OF RUNES HITS THE ICE

Your First Quests:

- ☞ Save the hockey team from Digger McGraw
- ☞ Find the secret of the tardigrades
- ☞ Go to the Ice Cap
- ☞ Find the Labyrinth of Doom

Your Starting Inventory:

- ➢ Hockey stick
- ➢ Photos of hockey heroes
- ➢ Memory of the Tower of Darkness world

The hockey mask on Digger McGraw's face gave him the look of a giant man-eating insect. Huge pimples on his nose glistened beneath the glow of the overhead rink lights. His eyes squinted, and drops of sweat beaded on the protruding ridges of the mask. He lifted the hockey stick over his head.

Chuck Farris swerved on his ice skates, barely missing Digger's body by about three inches. Chuck was heading for the boards. He crouched and careened past Digger in a hard right half-circle, and his friends in the stands rose and screamed, their eyes wide with terror. Melody Shaw's face was hidden in her mittens.

Josh Samson was jumping up and down, and pointing past Chuck to something on the ice.

What was it?

Chuck's body eased up, and he lifted his head and turned it slightly to the right, hoping to see whatever Josh was pointing at. Digger zoomed toward him, fast as lightning, crouched low, stick raised straight in the air.

Chuck wanted to scream, "*Penalty!* Get him for a penalty, Coach!"

But Coach Flanders was nowhere in sight. At least, he wasn't anywhere in Chuck's range of vision. All Chuck could see right now was the big, slimy, pimpled face of Digger McGraw. The scream of the kids in the stands surged and became a bonfire of noise. Chuck's vision blurred.

He ducked, just in time, as Digger's stick came crashing down past his left shoulder, almost skewering the ice. Digger was a terrific athlete, and he chortled as he quickly whooshed past Chuck in a tight circle, closing in again for the kill.

Where was Coach Flanders? Digger was trying to *kill* Chuck. This went way beyond an after-school hockey game, way beyond anything Chuck had ever experienced playing Major League Hockey for Poultrieville Middle and Senior High School. If Chuck had his way, Digger would be thrown off the team. It didn't matter that the guy was so good on skates. It only mattered that he didn't play fair, he was always after the kill, the pummeling of any poor slob on skates who wasn't fast enough to duck and streak away and hide from him.

A few blue jerseys zipped to view from Chuck's right, meaning that his teammates were coming: Al and Tony and Vince. Thank god. From the other side of the rink, however, came Digger's pals: his sidekick, the bully Jack Fastolf, and a few of *their* cronies. Four or five guys, in all, were closing in on Chuck. And they all looked mean and mad.

Chuck streaked down the ice between the two team ranks, down where the coach sat chatting with Mr. Viking, the janitor, and the principal, Mr. Calhoun. Why wasn't the coach paying attention? *Why?*

"Come on, little girl!" yelled Digger, circling Chuck and waving his stick. Digger raced down the ice past the boys in the center of the rink. The puck was somewhere in the jumble of bodies. What was up with the stupid bully, anyway? He should be after the puck, not after Chuck. It seemed that Digger McGraw existed just to give Chuck and his friends a hard time. When would the guy ever give it a rest and leave Chuck alone?

Someone—Al or Vince—shot the puck toward the goal, which was a few feet away from Digger, Jack Fastolf, and the goalie, a beefy six-footer named George Croute. George's family came from somewhere in France, and George was one hot hockey player. He could play any position really well. It was hard to slam a puck into the net whenever George played goal. On the other hand, it was great for the Poultrieville team to have George Croute on their side. It meant that Chuck's team usually beat other schools, statewide, because no matter how well the offense played for the other teams, they rarely could sink a goal in the Poultrieville net.

Wham!

Slashing, charging, spearing: Digger went wild with his hockey stick, stabbing Chuck in the arm and stomach, walloping him over the head, slamming him with that tall, fourteen-year-old body.

Chuck doubled over in pain. For a second, he hadn't been paying attention, and now he winced and dropped his stick and clutched his right arm where Digger's stick had slammed into him. *Chuck's arm was broken.* He had no feeling in his fingers, and his arm was stiff, numb, and burning with pain. He fell to the ice, trying not to cry. *He couldn't let Digger see him cry.* He wanted to stand up, grab his own hockey stick, and really go after Digger, but Chuck just wasn't like that: Chuck just wanted Digger to leave him alone, leave his friends alone, just leave them all alone . . .

Digger had flunked twice, and he was well known as the town bully. It wasn't fair that such a big bully was on a team with Chuck and other eighth graders. It wasn't even fair to let the guy play against George Croute, who was in tenth grade. Bullies like Digger McGraw and Jack Fastolf shouldn't be allowed to play team sports at all.

Digger laughed and pointed at Chuck. Jack Fastolf was laughing, too, and pointing at Chuck. Jack was becoming increasingly violent these days, taking after his longtime pal, Digger. Used to be Jack was the silent type, just following Digger's lead. Lately, though, since the Demon of Runes incident last November and

December, Jack had started setting kids' backpacks on fire and selling beer to little kids in elementary school. Rumor had it that someone, maybe Jack or Digger, was even selling drugs. Jack was old, like Digger, and had failed a few times. A wispy beard curled on his chin, and with all his thick blond hair and his blond moustache, the creep always reminded Chuck of the *Wizard of Oz* lion.

Now the lion was shoving guys like Vince and Al and George Croute, and skating closer with Digger to yell insults at Chuck.

"Look at the little mama's boy!"

"Ha ha! Look at the little girlie! Wimp wimp!"

"Big-time Video Boy, *huh*, Fruit Fly Boy, *huh*, stupid little baby boy!"

Chuck wanted to die.

George Croute grabbed Digger's hockey jersey and pushed him against Jack Fastolf. "Cut it out," said George. "Leave him alone. Go bully kids your own size."

Few people toyed with George Croute. It was certain suicide to get in George's way. Even Digger and Jack were afraid of George, and that fear now showed on both of their faces. Digger's laugh cracked a bit, and he frowned. Jack skated backward, and he raised his arms in a conciliatory gesture. "Hey, it's just a game, man," said Jack, his voice cracking high and then descending into the low, guttural, lion-like growl of a fourteen-year-old kid with a sprouting beard.

"No harm meant, dude," added Digger, also skating back toward the walkway to the locker room.

"Hockey's a tough sport, you know, man? You can't handle the grit, you get outta the rink."

"Yeah," said Jack.

The two bullies skated up the walkway, then disappeared into the murk of the locker room. Chuck could hear them laughing, even over the grumbling and the hoots of the crowd. He felt like a fool, with all his friends—the whole school—watching him, while he rolled in pain on the ice, flat on his back, now twisting to his side, clutching his right arm, moaning, trying to keep back tears.

George and Vince lifted Chuck by the waist and left shoulder. Chuck's vision was still blurred: everything flashed pink and blue, and then he shook his head, and the dizziness evaporated like steam off the ice.

"What's with *them*?" asked George with his French accent.

Vince shook his head. He was small and dark, with black hair and eyes. He was also tough and a great athlete, with muscles like rock. Chuck had known Vince for as long as he could remember. Vince said, "Digger's a jerk, George. He once stuck Josh's clothes down the toilet."

"And he crammed Styrofoam packing pellets down some kid's throat after school," said Chuck.

"And he tried to beat up Melody Shaw a few times, too," said Vince.

George grimaced. His blue eyes hardened, his lips tightened. "He beats up girls?" he said.

"Yup," said Chuck, rubbing his arm, which was beginning to thaw from the pain. He shook it a little, and it loosened further. Maybe it wasn't broken after all; it was probably just bruised badly, and, no doubt, it would be sore for at least a week. It was going to be tough to play in next week's game for the state semifinals. For crying out loud, that stupid Digger McGraw was such an idiot. You don't go around beating up your own team the week of a big game; it was just plain stupid. Chuck said, "Come on, guys, let's get out of here. I'm sick of talking about Digger and the lion."

"The lion?" said George.

"Jack Fastolf," Vince said.

George laughed, then clapped Chuck across the back lightly. "Oh, right," he said, nodding. "The *lion*. I get it. Mister King of the Jungle himself. Well, he shouldn't go around beating up girls."

Everyone knew that George Croute was a little sweet on Melody Shaw. Chuck really didn't understand the attraction, but he knew that Melody blushed a lot whenever George was around. Chuck supposed it was a good thing that George liked Melody, because then George would protect Melody the next time Digger and Jack went after her.

Chuck remembered very well the last time that happened. It was only a couple of months ago, back when Digger McGraw and Jack Fastolf almost destroyed Poultrieville Middle and Senior High School, and with it the whole town and everyone in it. Only Chuck and Digger remembered the entire incident: the Tower of Darkness world, the Demon of Runes, the pasty blue flowers on the edge of the vapor bridge, and all the rest of it. But everyone in town, and everyone in school, remembered the battles in the school halls and classrooms, how Chuck almost got kicked off the basketball team, how Chuck saved the town from the huge blizzard. Those had been very strange times.

Back in the locker room, Chuck pulled off his jersey, shorts, skates, socks, and underclothes. The locker room smelled bad, and it was dank with mold and rot. Inside Chuck's locker were photos of the Toronto Maple Leafs, the Buffalo Sabres, and the Rochester Americans. Chuck also had photos of Craig Charon and Jody Gage of the Rochester Americans, of Eric Lindros of the Philadelphia Flyers, of Scott Metcalfe and Wayne Gretzky. The photos gave him an extra lift before games, and they gave him a spark of energy after games.

Chuck wished for perhaps the millionth time that his father was still around to watch him play ice hockey, but he quickly cast aside the thought. Chuck's father was long gone. He'd run off with a bimbo store clerk, and he'd left Chuck and his mother, and their elderly cat, Schnooky, to fend for themselves on the highway outside of town. Chuck still didn't understand why his father didn't care, and he probably never *would* understand. His mother refused to talk about it.

Chuck twirled his lock three times, entered his combination, 24-2-9, and swung open the door. Beside him, George Croute was already slamming his own locker door shut and heading for the showers. "You coming, buddy?" he asked Chuck.

"Yeah," said Chuck . . . slowly.

"What's wrong?" asked George. He came closer, his hairy body smelling awful from the workout on the ice.

Chuck sucked in some air through his mouth so he could avoid smelling his friend. "My photos are gone," he said, "and in their place are these—these really *weird* drawings."

"Like what kinds of drawings?" George hitched his white towel up tighter around his waist and peered over Chuck's shoulder to get a better view of the locker door.

"Look at this, George. What does it mean?"

"I haven't a clue." George smoothed the hair down the back of his head. He had very long brown hair, and it was plastered with sweat to his scalp and shoulders. Usually, George's hair was thick and curly. He had curly brown hair on his shoulders, too, and his chest was thick with muscles. The guy looked like a worldwide wrestling champ.

Chuck remembered how his own body had changed back when he battled Digger and Jack in the Tower of Darkness world. The normal Chuck was five-foot-eleven, a born jock, with muscles, brawn, and a wide freckled face topped by bright red hair. That's how he thought of himself, anyway; but a few months ago, when the Demon of Runes emerged and gave Chuck video-game superhero powers, Chuck's entire body had grown to superhero proportions.

Before he knew it, Chuck had huge toe muscles, he could flatten doors with a fingertip, and his chest had hair all over it. He was able to leap to the ceiling, spring off the tiles, do flips, and land like a cat on the balls of his feet. His ribs were wider, his stomach solid with muscle, his chest bulging with strength. His fingers were like solid metal tubing, his nails thicker than bulletproof glass. He had felt giant rocks of muscle on his back, his upper arms, his thighs.

And then, all that had vanished after Chuck saved the town and the school from Digger McGraw, after Chuck restored the balance between the Tower of Darkness world and the real world. For a long time now, Chuck's body had been normal: a big, strapping normal, for sure, but still it was *normal.*

George Croute's normal physique, on the other hand, was that of a wrestling champion. *Good thing George is on our side,* thought Chuck. *The last thing the town needs is a brute like George teaming up with Digger McGraw and Jack Fastolf.*

A high-pitched voice piped up, "I know what that stuff means."

Chuck whirled, almost colliding with the mass of George's body. But the voice didn't come from George; rather, it came from Josh Samson, Chuck's best friend. Chuck laughed with relief. "Dude, you almost scared me to death."

"Sorry," said Josh, always the polite one.

George shrugged and turned toward the showers. "Well, this is all very interesting, about these drawings of yours, but tell me after I shower. I stink like garbage."

Josh and Chuck looked at each other. Neither one of them wanted to agree that George smelled like garbage—not to George's face, anyway. But as George lumbered into the shower room and the two boys heard the crank of the faucet wheels and the spray of water on the broken tiles, they screwed their noses into "Oh, that stinks" position and shuddered.

"Whew," said Josh, "I guess it's not such a bad thing to do homework instead of sports."

Chuck shook his head. "It's a good thing to play sports, Josh. Just look at your arm muscles, look at them." He pushed Josh's T-shirt sleeve up and gestured at his friend to make a muscle.

Josh turned a little pink, but he complied, squeezing his hand into a fist and creating a golf-ball-sized lump on his upper right arm. "It does look pretty cool," he said.

"You bet it does," said Chuck. "You didn't have that much muscle a few months ago. You keep lifting weights and working out like I showed you, Josh, and before you know it, you'll be playing hockey, too."

"I—I don't think so," said Josh. He dropped his arm and shoved his shirtsleeve back in place. "I'm better off sticking with chess."

Chuck disagreed, but he didn't want to push his friend. All of Josh's muscle power was in his brain. His shoulders were bones covered by skin. His chest was concave, his fingers built for computers and piano playing: he was essentially a brain on a stick. He'd had a hard time of it, battling the bullies in the Tower of Darkness world, but luckily Josh didn't remember any of it: only Chuck and Digger remembered the Tower of Darkness world.

Chuck figured it was a miracle that Josh played sports at all. It had taken Chuck years to get Josh to shoot hoops for fun, to lift weights, to get *some* exercise. In Chuck's opinion, exercise and sports were the keys to happiness. Chuck was most happy when he was scoring baskets for the team, slamming pucks into the goal, and outracing other kids in track. It wasn't so much the competition that he loved, though that *was* fun; rather, Chuck liked the feeling of sweating, panting, pushing himself to the limit.

Hopefully, Josh wouldn't need to use his muscles to save lives again. Hopefully, Chuck wouldn't have to be tortured with superhero powers again. At first, it had been fun, running that fast and leaping that high, but truth be known, Chuck Farris preferred being *only* Chuck Farris, ordinary kid. All those superhero muscles had gotten him into some pretty hot water.

Hopefully, the Demon of Runes was safe within his lair in the Tower of Darkness world. It wasn't that the Demon was a bad guy, but when he crossed into the real world, things got very strange—disrupted as if the energy of the planet changed. Even with superhero powers, Chuck doubted he could ever rise to the occasion again. He didn't want to find out.

Josh said, "You know, you still play too many sports, and you still do practically no homework."

"Well, when I need a second mother, I'll let you know," said Chuck. "But for now, one mother is more than enough, thanks very much."

"It's only fair. You're always whining at me about building up my muscles. I've always said you're a lot smarter than you think."

Chuck shrugged. "Uh-huh, well, maybe I'm just lazy. I do enough homework, Josh. *Really*." The thought of homework depressed him. He was still sweaty from the game, and his muscles ached. He needed a shower. He probably smelled as bad as George Croute, or worse. "I'm hitting the showers," he told Josh, "but stay here and tell me about the drawings when I get out."

"Sure," said Josh, smoothing his dark hair over his forehead. His hair was parted in the center. His glasses were held together with tape on the left side. They were black plastic with thick lenses that made his eyes look even larger and rounder than they really were. Chuck wondered why his friend didn't get his glasses fixed more often. The Samsons were really rich and lived in one of the nicest houses in Poultrieville. Josh's father was a lawyer; his mother helped in the law office sometimes, but other than that, she just stayed home and cooked amazing dinners and lunches. Josh was one lucky dude. He spent the summers reading comics in a lounge chair by his family's swimming pool. Chuck spent the summers mowing the ex-horse-pasture that pretended to be his lawn. By the highway was a three-hundred-yard-long ditch that was twenty feet deep. The ditch had to be mowed, too; it was half of Chuck's front yard.

Josh sat on the bench in front of Chuck's locker and twiddled with his sneaker laces. "No hurry," he said. "The drawings are all stupid junk like crossbones and funerary urns and the Danse Macabre."

"Say what?" said Chuck, turning back. Maybe his

ears were ringing and he wasn't hearing things correctly. After all, he'd just been clobbered on the ice.

"You heard me," said Josh. "These are all death symbols, Chuck. They're probably from Digger. I'd ignore them, if I were you. In fact, while you shower, I'll rip this junk off your locker and throw it away." Josh started ripping the drawings off the locker door.

"No, wait a minute," said Chuck. He grabbed Josh's wrist and took some papers from his friend's hand. He uncrumpled the papers and stared at them. "These are too well drawn to be from Digger."

"So he didn't draw them." Josh shrugged. "He got them from a book, or something. What's the big deal?"

Chuck spread a paper on the bench and sat down. George Croute was singing something in French from the shower room. The guy couldn't hold a tune. He was way off key. "Mademoiselle parlez vous hurrah hurrah" was what it sounded like, but then what the heck did Chuck know about French? Absolutely squat. "Mademoiselle parlez vous hurrah hurrah."

Well, Chuck knew bad singing when he heard it in *any* language, and he winced from the noise; but then something on the paper caught his eye, and the sound of George's voice dimmed and took on an eerie quality, as if the boy wasn't really in the shower singing at all, as if he was far away on a distant cliff, and only the echoes of his voice were permeating the dense clouds hanging over Chuck.

Chuck tried shaking his head, tried looking at the paper with clearer vision, but nothing helped. He pointed at the drawing, and his voice started trembling against his will. He could barely believe what he was seeing. "It's the Demon of Runes, Josh!"

"The *what*?"

"Don't you remember? The Demon of Runes. The guy I told you about!"

Josh sighed. "Yeah, I remember. Who could ever forget a story like that?"

"It wasn't a story. It happened!"

"Uh-huh. I know, buddy."

"Come on, Josh, I didn't make it up!" Chuck had told his friend all about their adventures in the Tower of Darkness world, but Josh had humored him, not believing it, telling Chuck that he should grow up to write science fiction and fantasy for a living. Fat chance. Chuck would grow up to play professional ice hockey or basketball, or maybe he'd be a self-employed, self-sufficient businessman of some kind, but he certainly wouldn't grow up to be a writer. "I didn't make it up," he repeated.

"I know, Chuck, just calm down. I believe you." Josh was attempting to look sincere and convincing, but Chuck wasn't buying any of it.

"Well, then, look at this!" cried Chuck, pointing to the paper on the bench. His friend lowered his eyes to focus on the drawing.

It wasn't a drawing, after all. Before their eyes, what had appeared to be a simple drawing of skeletons and oddball astrological-type symbols and urns and dancing crones was now a blurry photo. It had been shot in a dark room that had a glowing red ring in the middle of the floor. In the center of the ring was a big fiery kind of guy with huge muscles.

As if it was happening all over again, Chuck heard the fiery guy say, "I come from the Tower of Darkness. Where it exists, I exist."

Josh glanced sharply at Chuck. "Did you hear that, Chuck?"

"You heard it, too?" said Chuck.

Josh nodded, his face drained of all color.

"The Tower of Darkness exists only when space and time align a certain way, when someone gains certain skills at a certain time," said the Demon of Runes. He had warm red eyes and worm-like hair, but they were just ordinary rain worms, not the kind that ate people in horror movies. He wore a breechcloth rather than fighting armor. He carried no weapons. He just stood on the paper, flickering and wavering like a television video-game guy.

The Demon of Runes looked the same as he had looked on Chuck's television screen last December. He smiled and spread his arms. His fingers were long and bony and white. Yellow radiated from his nails. The yellow congealed, and Chuck felt a flush of power sweep down his body.

"Oh, Josh, it's happening again!" he cried. He didn't *want* to get involved in all this again, he *didn't want it*. And yet, when the Demon of Runes had called to him the first time, Chuck had been forced to obey the Demon and play by his rules. He had no choice back then, and somehow Chuck knew he would have no choice this time. The Demon of Runes maintained the barrier between the real world and the Tower of Darkness world, a strange place that Chuck,

Melody Shaw, and Josh Samson had entered by accident; and then they had been forced to battle Digger McGraw and Jack Fastolf, along with a pile of giant creatures and monsters, to save the real world from the Darkness.

Josh shoved his glasses up on his nose. That's what he always did when he was nervous or scared. He shifted on the bench, crossed his legs. His fingers were twitching. "Chuck, I'm scared," he said. "This isn't something Digger could have put in your locker. He can't create something like this, something that moves on a piece of paper—nobody can do something like that, certainly not an idiot like Digger McGraw."

On the paper, the photo was dimming, then brightening.

"Do you believe me now?" asked Chuck. "About the Demon of Runes and the Tower of Darkness? *Do you believe me?*"

His friend nodded, fear and disbelief in his eyes. "I—I guess so, but I don't know, Chuck. I don't understand what you're talking about, or what this thing here *is* . . ."

It's the Demon of Runes, Chuck wanted to shout, but he controlled his temper and clenched his fists until the nails dug into the palms of his hands.

The voice penetrated the locker room again: "*Go to the Real Ice, Chuck Farris, go to the very Ice Cap of your world. There you will find the entrance to my lair.* There you will find a way to save me from my enemies, those who would destroy my world and, with it, your world and all its people. Find the Labyrinth of Doom, Chuck. Find it in the Real Ice. Look for the tardigrades. They are the key. *Save me from them, save me . . .* "

On the bench, the photo was dimming again, and the Demon of Runes spread his arms, and more yellow radiated from him, flushing straight down Chuck's body into his toes. Chuck staggered back against his metal locker, clanging the door shut.

"What's that?" yelled George from the showers.

"N-nothing," stammered Josh.

"Say *what*?"

"Nothing!" yelled Chuck, and his fingers were splayed behind him on the locker door.

"Okay, okay, don't get so excited about everything!" yelled George, and he went back to his singing.

Chuck's shoulders hunched down, but his back, still sweaty from the hockey game, clung to the metal locker, keeping him upright. His toes were supercharged with energy, or so it seemed, and he felt that, if he wanted to, he could easily leap to the ceiling and destroy it with the jab of one tiny toe.

Of course, he did nothing of the kind. He wasn't that kind of guy. Chuck didn't cause trouble, he was just an ordinary guy who slinked by with his grades, getting B's for the most part, and not standing out in any particular way. He preferred blending into the crowd, he didn't want teachers spreading glory all over him—that was embarrassing stuff. Chuck was an average guy, except when it came to sports, that is. There, Chuck *ruled*.

"Chuck, it's gone," whispered Josh.

Chuck forced himself to look at the paper on the bench. Just as Josh said, the Demon of Runes was gone. In his place on the paper was a photo of Scott Metcalfe of the Rochester Americans.

Your Quest Journal:

1. Save the hockey team from Digger McGraw: FAILURE.
2. Find the secret of the tardigrades: FAILURE.
3. Go to the Ice Cap: FAILURE.
4. Find the Labyrinth of Doom: FAILURE.

Your Inventory:

- Hockey stick
- Photos of hockey heroes
- Memory of the Tower of Darkness world
- Photo of Scott Metcalfe and the Demon of Runes

NHL 2001: GAME OVER. CONTINUE?

SSX SNOWBOARDING: GAME OVER. CONTINUE?

SUMMONER: GAME OVER. NEW GAME?

TIMESPLITTERS: BEGIN NEW GAME?

THE BOUNCER: BEGIN NEW GAME?

Special Bonus! Chuck Farris Presents Hot NHL 2001 Tips

Are any of you guys out there hockey fans? Well, if you haven't guessed yet, I am. If you like to play and watch hockey, then you'll also enjoy the PlayStation2 game called NHL 2001. It's a lot like real hockey on the ice.

Let me tell you some stuff about hockey and NHL 2001, and why I thought the coach should have given Digger McGraw a penalty.

In hockey, there are three periods of play, and each period is exactly twenty minutes long. If the score is tied at the end of three periods, then the game goes into a fourth or overtime period. This special period is up to five minutes long, and each time it plays with one less player. When a goal is scored, the game is over.

Excluding the goalie, each hockey team has five men on the ice. The "center" is responsible for the face-offs, when the referee drops the puck and the two centers try to gain control of it. In addition to the center, each team has right and left "wingers," who work with the center to serve as the team's offense. Finally, the two defensemen try to stop the enemy guys from scoring goals.

The goalie guards the net. Goals are scored by getting the puck past the goalie and into the net that he's guarding.

Although there are three twenty-minute periods, each game usually takes two to three hours. This is because the ice gets rough after each period, so some guy on a Zamboni makes the ice smooth. They give the guy eighteen minutes to clean up the ice using his Zamboni. He has to "Zamboni the ice" after warm-up, after the first period, and then after the second and third periods. The clock also stops every time a penalty is called, which takes up more time.

This subject, penalties, brings us to Digger McGraw. You'd think the coach would have thrown him out of the game, and even off the team, wouldn't you? At minimum, the creep should have gotten a penalty.

There are several types of penalties in hockey: minors, majors, ten-minute misconduct, and game (or a couple of games) misconduct. Minor penalties are two minutes long. Some examples of a minor penalty are tripping, high-sticking, slashing, boarding, hooking, and holding the stick of some guy on the other team. There's also a minor penalty for roughing, or picking fights with, other players.

Double minors keep a player (like Digger) out of the game for four minutes. Double minors happen when a player gets two penalties at once, like slashing a guy and then tripping him. Double minors are also given when a player spears someone (hits with the front of the stick) or butt-ends him (hits with the back of the stick).

Well, so far, all of these penalties seem to apply to Digger McGraw, wouldn't you say? I mean, this is a guy who once stuffed Candy Malone, a sixth grader, into a garbage bin—just for kicks! He's the last kind of guy we should have on a school sports team, and when he goes out of his way to beat up guys on the ice—

Well, the guy *really* annoys me.

But let me continue.

During a minor penalty, if somebody on the non-penalized team scores a goal, then the time on the guy's minor penalty will automatically expire, and he will be allowed to leave the penalty box. During a double minor, if somebody on the opposing team scores a goal, things get more complicated. For example, if there are two minutes and one second left on the penalty clock of somebody with a double minor, and then a guy—on the other team *only*—scores a goal, the time will go down to exactly two minutes. If the time remaining on the penalty is one minute and fifty-nine seconds, and someone on the other team scores a goal, then the penalty clock moves to zero and the penalized player can rejoin the game.

A major penalty is five minutes long. Major penalties are usually given if a player starts fighting and draws blood, or if a player slashes somebody's face really badly. (If you haven't guessed or you didn't already know, hockey is a very rough game.) The other team can score as many goals as they want during a major penalty without the guy ever getting out until his time expires. Ten-minute penalties are the same. And if two players fight, and the fight is a nasty one, the players may be thrown out of the game, or they may even be thrown out of the next couple of games.

When somebody gets a penalty, the other team has what's known as a power play. It's a power play because the penalized team has one less player on the ice. If two people on the same team are penalized, then the other team has a two-man advantage.

So let's say the coach happened to notice Digger and Jack Fastolf beating me up with their sticks, spearing me in the guts, tripping me, and breaking my arm. My guess is that *the coach should have given them both double penalties, but not major penalties*—because I wasn't bleeding. On the other hand, you don't really have to cause bleeding to get ten-minute penalties or game misconduct penalties. They should have been tossed into the penalty box.

We'll return to this later, but for now

I have to get out of the locker room—

Chuck Farris

2

MELODY SHAW SPLITS TIME

Your New Quests:

- ☞ Teach Melody some video-game basics
- ☞ Learn how to control time
- ☞ Unlock the tenth level
- ☞ Get an escort to Greenland

Josh picked up the photo and turned it over; then he peered closely at it, even taking off his glasses to examine it an inch from his face. "It's an ordinary photo, Chuck. The weird fiery guy is gone." Josh handed the Scott Metcalfe photo to Chuck.

Chuck turned, opened his locker, and stared at the inside of the door. All of his usual photos were back in place: the Toronto Maple Leafs, the Buffalo Sabres, and the Rochester Americans; photos of Craig Charon and Jody Gage of the Rochester Americans, and of Wayne Gretzky. Where the Scott Metcalfe photo usually hung, there were pieces of tape holding nothing to the door. Chuck slipped the Metcalfe photo back in place and closed his locker, leaning against it.

"What did the fiery guy mean by Real Ice and the Ice Cap, Chuck?"

Chuck had no clue. He shook his head. "I don't

know," he said. "I sure can't go anywhere, and neither can you. We're stuck here in school until June, and it's only January now. Besides, I can't go to the Ice Cap, even after school lets out. That's ridiculous." Inside, his thoughts were whirling: *If only I had Josh's brains, then I'd understand what the Demon of Runes meant by going to the Ice Cap and to the Real Ice; but I don't have Josh's brains, and I'm just not smart enough to figure this out. Josh may say I'm smarter than I think, but I'm inside this head, and I know that I don't understand how a photo turns into an eerie video clip of the Demon of Runes.*

Josh was fingering the narrow belt on his jeans. Then he fingered the PlayStation2 logo on his T-shirt. Then he poked his glasses up on his nose and gave Chuck a cross-eyed-owl look. "I bet there's a back-door way into this Ice Cap place, Chuck, just like there was a way into the Tower of Darkness place—or so you told me, anyway."

"Uh-huh," said Chuck, as if he'd already figured it out. Josh really was a *Brain*. "So I don't have to go to the *real* Ice Cap, do I?"

Josh shook his head back and forth, and mouthed the word *No-o-o . . .*

"I just have to find a way into the other place, the Ice Cap place, right?"

Josh shook his head up and down, and mouthed the word *Yes-s-s . . .*

Chuck looked blankly at his best friend. "And, of course, I haven't a clue where this Ice Cap place might be," he said.

"Neither do I," said Josh.

"Maybe I can help," said George Croute, coming up from behind them, water sloshing all over the locker-room floor and dripping from his hairy shoulders.

Chuck explained the situation, but George just sighed and shook his head. He didn't have a clue where to look for the Ice Cap place, either. And the looks he was giving both Chuck and Josh indicated that he didn't believe them, anyway. Chuck really couldn't blame the guy. What sane person would believe that a photo of Scott Metcalfe had just been a video of the Demon of Runes, who told Chuck to save him using tardigrades at the Ice Cap?

The boys called it a day and walked home. Josh and George both lived about two minutes away from school in the village. Chuck waved goodbye to them and made his way, alone, down the highway outside of town.

As usual, in the dead of winter in upstate New York, it was freezing cold, and the low gray hood of the sky threatened to dump snow and ice at any minute. It was getting late, and Chuck's mother would be home soon from her job at the dentist's office in the city. Luckily, she'd forced Chuck to wear his gloves and a hat today. He usually ignored her pleas to dress warmly, but this morning she was a bit sick, and Chuck had felt sorry for her, so he wore the gloves and hat to make her happy. He wondered how she'd done all day, working downtown while sick.

Chuck plodded along the highway, stopping whenever a gravel-pit truck zoomed past, so he wouldn't be blown into the ditch by the edge of the road. Chuck didn't understand why adults liked to speed, especially when ice and snow covered the roads. He hunched his shoulders and then shook them back, hitching his backpack into a more comfortable position. The swamp to the right was filled with snow and capped with ice. The swamp to the left looked the same. Next to each swamp was a spooky old house. The one on the right belonged to Candy Malone, a sixth grader who lived with her grandparents.

As he slopped through the ice and snow past her house, Chuck remembered how nice Candy had been to him during the Tower of Darkness nightmare. He smiled briefly. Good old Poultrieville. It sucked living on the highway, but at least he knew everyone both inside and outside town. Even knowing that a little kid like Candy Malone lived here by the swamp was kind of comforting.

Chuck didn't know why it was comforting, he just knew it was. Maybe if a gravel-pit truck knocked him into the ditch and crushed one of his legs, he could crawl up the hill past the swamp to Candy's house, and they'd know who he was, and they wouldn't call the cops, thinking Chuck was a burglar; instead, they'd help him, simply because everyone knew everyone both inside and outside town.

A truck flew past, careening and tottering on its wheels as if it was going to fall over. Speeding trucks often fell over on the highway, especially up ahead near Chuck's house, where a narrow country road intersected with the main road. Chuck shuddered as a spray of dirty ice blasted from the truck's wheels and hit him. He hunched lower to maintain his body warmth. His right arm hurt from where Digger's hockey stick had speared him. He jiggled his backpack again, this time to shift the weight more to his left shoulder. He'd be awfully glad to get home, where it was warm and light, and where he could eat some dinner.

He skirted past the large snowdrifts by the ditch in front of Melody Shaw's house. From Melody's front window came light, and through the wispy lace curtains, Chuck saw Melody and her mother setting the table for dinner. Melody was lucky, too; maybe not as lucky as Josh Samson, but lucky nonetheless. Her parents still lived together, and Melody was an only child, so she got plenty of attention and everything she wanted: nice clothes, new shoes, fine dinners. Her mother even drove her to school every morning. Her father fixed their plumbing and sewage tank, stuff that Chuck always had to do. Her father also mowed their part of the old horse pasture.

Chuck would be in the gravel driveway, working on his hand mower, trying to get it running, peering at its underside while clutching a bottle of oil, and out would trot Melody Shaw's father to sit high on his ride-on mower and cut three-foot-wide paths of grass so fast—why, so fast that Chuck would still be kicking the hand mower and wrenching back the start cord when Mr. Shaw finished and went inside for a cold brew.

He sighed, remembering, thankful that the winters were long and hard up here, cutting the mowing season way down.

He turned up his driveway, still worrying about what had happened after the hockey game. Was it possible that Digger McGraw had found another way into the Tower of Darkness, where the Demon of Runes lived? Had Digger found an entrance to—why, the idea was ludicrous—*Greenland*? The previous way into the Tower of Darkness, through the top floor of the school, specifically on a desk in the Mentoring Programs room, had been sealed off when Chuck returned to the real world last month. Chuck had taken the desk and burned it in the woodstove in his living room. For a month, he'd been relaxing, not worrying at all about Digger getting back into the Tower of Darkness and causing trouble again.

So how was Digger getting back into the Demon's world and causing trouble? Was Digger eating the pasty blue flowers that had the chemical composition of Industrial Strength Bug-Off? Was he beating really hot video games while snorting Bug-Off? Just what was the creep doing? The only way Chuck knew to get into the Tower of Darkness was to beat a game like Summoner, and then leap off the now-defunct desk in the Mentoring Programs room.

Chuck remembered:

All he had to do was beat Summoner, or any other video game, and he'd return to the Tower of Darkness. He'd read it on the walls. He'd read it, because the Demon of Runes wanted Chuck to keep his Tower of Darkness safe from creeps like Digger McGraw and Jack Fastolf.

Someone has to protect me from them, the Demon

had written. *They'll fry their brains on Bug-Off and get here by beating some games. I can't stop that. But you're the best, Chuck Farris.*

"It's you against me, Chuckie boy," Digger McGraw had said. "If I return to the Tower of Darkness, you'll have no choice but to follow."

Chuck shook his head to erase the memories. It gave him the creeps to remember what Digger and Jack had done to Chuck, to Josh, to Melody, and to the school. He remembered how scared Josh had been, and he remembered saying to Josh, "Don't let that bully scare you. I can beat him anytime, and you know it."

But could he?

If not for the Demon of Runes, all hell would break loose in Poultrieville, and for all Chuck knew the whole planet would go up in flames or something. Chuck really wasn't that big a hero. He'd only been able to beat Digger and Jack last time because the Demon of Runes gave him special powers.

The poor Demon of Runes, what a nice guy, and alone forever in the Tower of Darkness, living inside his own heart and his own body, never to escape, never to have a friend like Josh Samson, just living alone forever. The demon who lived in all video games but was from no particular video game. The demon who believed in fairness and honesty and justice. The demon who fought all the bad guys in all the video games of all time . . .

Whenever Chuck beat a PlayStation2 game, the Demon of Runes pushed him to a higher level of video-game play. He pushed him to such a high level that Chuck *became* the video-game superhero. He became all video-game superheroes smashed together in his one Chuck Farris body. And he possessed all of their inventories and weapons, their bravado, their mannerisms, and yet he possessed items and weapons and mannerisms that had nothing to do with video games. Everything was part reality and part video-game fantasy.

The only way to stop it all was for Chuck to make the active choice *not* to beat any video games. By not beating them, Chuck had given up all his superhero powers, his inventory, his weapons. In return, the Demon of Runes was imprisoned forever in his Tower of Darkness world. He couldn't come out of his world, and all that Darkness couldn't seep into reality.

As he twisted his key in the door lock, Chuck almost laughed. He had to use a key to get inside the house. At times like this, he wouldn't mind having some of his old Summoner video-game powers: it used to be that all Chuck had to do was mutter some Spanish phrase, and doors would open—or just fall off their hinges—without keys.

Oh, well. It was better to use a key than mutter a spell and be fighting off Digger McGraw and Jack Fastolf on a vapor bridge, with the sky pressing down on your head.

"Chuck?"

Ouch. He banged his hurt arm against the door. He whirled and almost fell off the tiny front porch. "Oh, Melody, geesh, this keeps happening to me today.

Josh almost scared me to death at school. What's up?"

Melody was shivering. "Can we go inside? It's cold out here."

"Sure." He opened the door so she could enter first, and then he followed her into the living room. He switched on the pole lamp by the door, and the room flooded with light.

Melody settled onto the sofa; it was green with blue and pink flowers. Chuck's mother had made the sofa cushions when he was a baby.

"Is something wrong?" Chuck asked, as he pulled off his coat, hat, and gloves, and put them all into the closet by the door. He wondered again what Melody was doing at his house. He'd just seen her setting the dinner table at home with her mother.

"No. Not at all." Melody glanced at him, then turned her attention toward the television screen across from the sofa. "My mother said I could come by here tonight. I just finished dinner, so she said I could come now."

"Oh. You just *finished* dinner," said Chuck. Apparently, he'd seen Melody and her mother clearing the dinner debris, not setting the table. "But why did you want to come over, Melody?" She rarely stopped by to see Chuck, now that they were all grown up in the eighth grade. He'd never hear the end of it if one of the guys happened to go by the house and see a girl in the living room. He hurried to the front window and drew the blinds shut.

She chuckled, as if knowing what he was trying to hide from the world. "Oh, Chuck, nobody's going to care if I come over here to see you. Besides, we live on a stupid highway, and only cars and trucks ever go past this place, and you know as well as I do that they're always speeding at sixty-five miles an hour."

True enough. But still, why was she here? Suddenly, he wondered instead what she had eaten for dinner. He was starving. Before he could eat, Chuck had to start a fire in the woodstove. The house always had a chill to it when he came home from school. So he placed some kindling sticks into the potbellied stove and lit them. Soon he'd add wood, and perhaps within half an hour the place would be warm.

"Listen, I have to make something to eat," he said, moving toward the short hallway leading to the kitchen. "I hope you don't mind. You want anything?"

"Just some water. I just ate, remember?" Melody smoothed back her hair, which was still short from when the beast had slashed it off in the Tower of Darkness world. Of course, she didn't remember being there, so she still didn't remember who or what had cut her hair, which used to hang to her waist. She followed him into the kitchen. She was wearing pink jeans and a long-sleeved tan sweater. She always wore very feminine clothes. She even had bangles—green and tan ones—on her wrists, and a sparkling barrette in her hair.

Chuck was uneasy. He didn't know why he was uneasy, it was just that most guys in eighth grade didn't have friends who were girls. He fumbled with the drawers, pulled some forks and knives from them, a spoon. He got a glass—no, two glasses—and filled both with water from the laundromat jugs. Nobody could drink the well water out here on the highway; instead, everyone filled empty milk jugs at the local laundromat.

"Cheers," said Melody, giggling slightly.

Chuck nodded, dumbfounded. He sipped some water, still staring at her, puzzled. Then he turned and pulled a plate and bowl from the cabinet by the sink. "Peanut butter and jelly?" he asked. "Maybe an apple?"

"No thanks, Chuck," Melody said. "Is that what you eat for dinner?"

"Afraid so," he said, smearing goo on some stale white bread slices.

"That's disgusting."

No kidding.

"Don't you eat the same thing for lunch every day, too?"

He turned, smiled broadly, then crammed half a sandwich into his mouth and chewed. He kept smiling, pretending it was delicious. How could someone like Melody Shaw understand that (a) Chuck's mother worked constantly, and when she wasn't working, she didn't have the energy to fix roast beef and mashed potato dinners, or chocolate cakes; (b) Chuck didn't know how to cook anything, so he usually ate peanut butter and jelly sandwiches for dinner; and (c) when he wasn't eating peanut butter and rotting apples, he was eating Cap'n Crunch cereal?

Melody sipped some more laundromat water and sat at the kitchen table, giving him a look that said

Oh, you poor boy, eating such trash for lunch and dinner. He half-hoped she'd offer to bring him leftovers from her house.

No such luck, but she did say, "Maybe my mother will let you come for dinner tomorrow night. Would you like that?"

Yes. "No," he said, feeling heat in his cheeks.

She glowered at him.

"What I mean—"

"I know, Chuck. It wouldn't look good if a girl had you over for dinner. Like anyone would even find out. Oh, well, have it your way. But don't say I didn't ask."

"Maybe sometime," he said. "Thanks, Melody."

She rolled her eyes, as if thinking *Boys are so dumb.* Chuck crammed the rest of the sandwich in his mouth and turned to the counter to make another. This time, he'd use strawberry jam, just for something different.

If only his mother believed in having something different, but no, Chuck's mother was high on keeping everything the same: the food, the water, the house, the color of the walls, the furniture, the rugs. "I want stability in my life," she always said. "I want to know that some things will always be the same."

But there had to be limits! Like the living room, their kitchen was green: the walls, the tile floor, the countertops, the curtains by the table. The table itself was wood, but it had two green placemats on it. Chuck's mother was obsessed with green. All the walls in the entire house were painted light green: even the walls in Chuck's bedroom. Sometimes, it drove him batty.

"If I do it all one color—for example, green," his mother would say, "then I won't have to worry about wasting paint, and I won't have to worry that something doesn't match." Chuck had to admit that there was some logic to his mother's love of green.

" . . . *Greenland.*" Melody had just said something, and it had to do with green.

He blinked. *"Greenland?"* he said, turning from the counter with two cheekfuls of strawberry jam and peanut butter.

"Yeah, I want to play TimeSplitters with you, Chuck. I want you to show me how to create a really cool maze and make it all icy-like so I can pretend that I'm racing through underground ice mazes in Greenland."

"Oh, man, so that's why you're here! You want to play TimeSplitters? Excellent." His mood lifted. Melody was one cool girl. She'd come to play video games with him on the PlayStation2. Of course!

Forget the apple and stale sandwiches. Chuck headed straight back into the living room, where he plopped onto the sofa, Melody beside him, and he cranked up the PlayStation2. Chuck was the videogame king of Poultrieville. He could outplay anyone with video games, even Digger McGraw, who ranked number two in town.

He slipped the TimeSplitters disk into the console and showed Melody around the game, explaining the controls and the levels as he went. He let her try things out, too, so she could choose how she wanted to play: story mode or arcade mode. "You should get used to the arcade mode first," he recommended, "before you try beating story mode or creating your own mazes."

"But I don't want to wait. I want to make a really neat maze," she said.

Melody could be a pain, but Chuck also knew that she could be one amazing fighter when push came to shove. She was made of far more grit than she remembered. He had doubted her ability to help him during their Summoner exploits in the Tower of Darkness, yet Melody had come through with shining glory: she could outfence and outmaneuver bacites and brass golems.

"I'll show you how to make a maze, but I have to show you other stuff first," he insisted. "And by the way, what's this business about Greenland? Does that happen to be where the Ice Cap is located?" He hoped that he sounded naïve and innocent.

She laughed, scooping up the second controller from the floor. "Sure, the Ice Cap's in Greenland. Where have *you* been? Miss Olivia taught us about Greenland last month."

"Yeah, well, I was kind of occupied in December, remember?"

She cocked an eyebrow. "Yeah, sure I remember. You almost got kicked off the basketball team and thrown out of school for infesting it with fruit flies." Then she added, "But, of course, you ended up being a big hero and everything."

"Let's get back to the video games, okay? I don't want to talk about that stuff anymore."

"Sure, Chuck," she said, and so they settled back

onto the sofa and played for a couple of hours. Time drifted past, the cat drifted into the living room and out again—four times—and more time drifted past. The cat raced around the living room, chasing house screws and batting them into a pile near the front door. Chuck stoked the fire three or four times . . .

The evening drifted along, and they split the television screen in two, so Melody could play one half and Chuck could play the other. By 8 PM, Chuck's mother still wasn't home from work. Chuck wouldn't worry—not yet—because maybe the roads were shut down on the freeway, or maybe a truck had fallen over on the ice, blocking the main route. He'd give his mother until nine; then he'd really start worrying about where she was and whether she was okay. In the meantime, he'd play video games with Melody.

He showed her how to beat the first three levels of TimeSplitters so she could unlock the next three levels. They swept through the tomb, the Chinese zone, and the cyberden. Chuck had to help her a lot, but he was anxious to move her into the harder zones, where they could have more fun together.

Adventure music blared from the television. It fit perfectly with the blast-'em adventures of the game. "Duck!" Chuck yelled, and Melody's character, Captain Ash, ducked behind a wall. "Now hop back into view again!" Melody's character leapt from behind the wall. A skeleton robot guy followed her character. "Now get him, Melody, get him!" She let loose with her tommy gun, and the skeleton robot guy exploded into bits.

Finally, Melody got the ankh, the whole point of this level, and a pile of timesplitters and skeletons appeared out of nowhere and attacked her. "Run!" yelled Chuck, and her character started streaking this way and that past ancient Egyptian paintings and candles on the tomb walls. She jumped over boxes, and over holes in the floor, where skeletons paced below in a subterranean dungeon. Giant blue energy balls erupted all over the place, followed by blasts of green energy balls. Melody ducked, dodged, and ran, avoiding the green blasts and making her way to safety, to the red circle at the end of the level.

Both of them hooted and clapped their hands. Melody had beaten a maze level of TimeSplitters, a really hard game, and she'd done it all by herself!

"You're *good*!" said Chuck. He'd almost forgotten she was a girl.

"I want to do arcade mode, and I want to beat red aliens and lumberjacks and robofish, too! And look, I want to play a siamese cyborg and a—"

"Okay, okay, just calm down, there's plenty of time, you just learned how to play this game. It's hard."

He sat back in awe as she flew through the Chinese level, through the kitchens and bathrooms, past the red aliens; as she shattered the windows everywhere; as the gong banged; as bad guys suddenly appeared in balls of yellow flame. She shattered all the plates in the kitchen. She destroyed the wok.

"Hey, calm down."

Her face was totally focused on the screen. Her

eyes didn't waver. She seemed not to hear him. She ran through the gardens, through the alleys, into the basement. She ran past bookshelves and tables. And she won awards—

For Most Manic and for Fists of Fury.

Then Melody got stuck, trying to beat the village, the chemical plant, and planet-x. "And," said Chuck, "there are three more levels, too, after you beat these three. The mansion, the docks, and the spaceways."

"So when do I get to make my own maze, Chuck? I want to make a maze of Greenland."

He laughed. "How about tomorrow after school? You can practice some more, and then I'll help you make a maze of your own."

"Oh, wow! Thanks, Chuck!" Melody's face was glowing with happiness. "You're the greatest!"

Greenland. The Ice Cap. Tardigrades. The Demon of Runes. "Say, Melody," said Chuck, "have you ever heard of a tardigrade?"

She shook her head. "No. Sorry, Chuck, but you can ask Josh Samson. He's a brain. He knows everything."

"I don't think Josh knows what it means, either."

"Look it up on the Internet."

"My mom doesn't have the Internet."

"Well, my parents have the Internet, so I'll look it up for you when I get home tonight. How do you spell it?" She concentrated, repeating the letters after him.

"Call me when you get home, and tell me, would you?"

"Sure, but what's the big deal?"

"I don't know, to tell you the truth. Some guy was talking to me today about tardigrades and the Ice Cap, that's all."

"You always have been the mysterious one, Chuck." She slipped into her coat, pushed on her hat, pulled on her gloves, and headed for the door. "Thanks again for the fun. I hope your mother gets home okay."

Yeah, so did Chuck. He watched Melody slide down the driveway toward the highway; then he shut the door as she walked past the fence post that served as a marker between their houses. He returned to the television set and the PlayStation2 console. The screen was still split, but somehow it was now split into four small windows rather than two. Melody's character was in each small window, contemplating the same red alien. But in the top left window, her character held a club and was two feet shorter than the red alien, and in the top right window, her character had a wad of dynamite and weighed about five hundred pounds and stood only two feet tall.

Chuck peered at the bottom two windows, which held equally bizarre morphs of Melody's basic character. One clutched a broken wok, and the other was reading a textbook called *Greenland's Underground Delights*. Pretty weird, thought Chuck. These characters always look the same in this game. There's no way to change them into five-hundred-pound guys, for example; and how did Melody get the screen to split like this all of a sudden?

Maybe there was a glitch in the electricity or in the television itself. Chuck turned everything off, then turned it back on. The video game was fine, as was the television screen. No weird five-hundred-pound guys lumbering around with clubs and dynamite, nobody reading textbooks or clutching broken woks.

Schnooky, Chuck's ancient cat, followed him into the kitchen, where he checked the time: nine o'clock. Where *was* his mother? The cat lapped some water from her bowl, sniffed her chow, then curled up by his feet. She was seventeen years old, which was really old for a cat. Her fur wasn't as shiny as it had been when Chuck was in kindergarten, and her eyes weren't as bright and innocent, either. But Schnooky was faithful and loyal, and always kept him company when his mother had to work late, or during school holidays, when Chuck was home alone.

He was home alone most of the time.

He didn't like it very much.

He picked up the cat, and she whined, and he carried her into the living room, where he sat on the sofa again. And that's when the phone rang. He dumped the cat to the floor, and she howled at the bad treatment; he raced back to the kitchen and grabbed the phone.

It was Melody Shaw. "About those tardigrades—"

"Yes?"

"Yeah, well, I looked it up on my mother's laptop. They're really cute, actually."

"Melody, what do they *do*? What's the big deal about them?"

"Hold on, Chuck, I'm getting to it. Be patient," said Melody.

He kept his mouth shut. The tardigrades were one part of the puzzle that made absolutely no sense to him at all. He was anxious to solve all the puzzle pieces, all at once, if possible, but he knew that he'd have to be patient. "Okay, Melody, go on and tell me everything you learned about the tardigrades. I'll keep quiet, I promise."

She paused, apologized briefly for snapping at him, and then she explained: "Chuck, tardigrades are microscopic animals that can survive long-term freezing. They live in places like Greenland inside the Ice Cap."

They survive long-term freezing. They're microscopic.

Melody continued: "It says here that when Leeuwenhoek invented the microscope a few hundred years ago, one of the first animals he happened to see was the tardigrade, and people gave the tardigrade special names like moss piglet and water bear, and even teddy bear. *Tardi* means slow. *Grado* means walker. The tardigrade lumbers around slowly, and he does look really cute, like I said. The picture on the Internet shows a tardigrade with six fat legs on each side of his fat body, and a teddy-bear face with a tube mouth for eating algae."

Wind hit the house. The roof and shutters rattled. Ice was blasting down: Chuck could hear it hammering the roof. The cat was howling somewhere in the rear of the house, probably in Chuck's room beneath the bed. The phone started crackling.

Quickly, before the phone might die, he asked

Melody how the tardigrade managed to survive long-term freezing.

Melody's voice dimmed, returned, and dimmed again. The phone line was going. She said, "The tardigrades have evolved so they can be frozen time and time again, Chuck. It's not that they can avoid being frozen solid. Their blood has ice-nucleating agents in it. These are special kinds of molecules that encourage the growth of ice crystals inside the tardigrade. Lemme see, this is all kind of complicated."

Chuck was already baffled by most of what Melody had told him. "Do the animals have some kind of antifreeze? Is that what you're saying?"

"Well, that, too. Yeah, they do produce antifreeze of some kind, and they also produce a protecting chemical that keeps their body cells from rupturing as they freeze and get dehydrated. Listen, Chuck, the rest of the Internet article is gobbledegook to me. I don't understand it."

The line was crackling like crazy.

Look for the tardigrades. They are the key. That's what the Demon of Runes had told Chuck in the locker room.

Chuck thanked Melody for her help, and hung up the phone. He had to keep the line open in case his mother called from downtown. And just as he'd hoped, a moment later the phone rang again, and this time it *was* his mother. She was fine, but she was trapped in the dentist's office for the night. The roads leading from the city were closed.

"Turn on the news," she said, and her voice sounded

terrified. It was all high-pitched and squeaky, very much unlike his mother's usual voice, which was calm and peaceful. "There are dead ends all over town, Chuck. And I mean *everywhere*."

"What do you mean, Mom? Dead ends? How so?"

Her voice rose a notch. "I mean *dead ends*! I went down Main Street, where I usually get on the freeway to come home, and Main Street dead-ended. It just stopped! There was a big wall there, right before the corner of Main and Jefferson, and the wall went so high into the sky that I couldn't see the top of it."

He took the receiver from his ear and stared at it. "Is this some kind of joke?" he said. "Who are you, anyway? This is *not* funny."

"I'm your *mother*, Chuck! I'm telling you to turn on the news. Go! Now! I'll wait here. Don't hang up the phone."

He muttered something, then did as she told him. He turned on the television and pressed the numbers to display the local news station. There was no nine o'clock news. He rolled his eyes toward the ceiling.

He returned to the phone. "Mom, there *is* no news on at this hour."

"Go back and wait for some!" she practically shrieked.

"Okay, okay . . ."

He sat on the sofa, feeling stupid, for what seemed like fifteen minutes. A sitcom about two guys and three girls in the glamorous modeling business was airing. Boring, boring, boring.

And then: "We interrupt this program to bring you

an important and shocking news development affecting the city and all surrounding towns."

Chuck sat forward, his elbows on his knees, hardly believing what he heard.

"The mayor has declared the city closed until further notice. Do not attempt to get into the city. If you're already in the city, do not attempt to leave."

Say what?

A camera was jostling down Main Street toward Jefferson, and to his horror Chuck saw the huge wall his mother had mentioned. It did indeed rise so high into the sky that he couldn't see the top of it.

"And everywhere in the city, we're finding one dead end after another. Officials estimate that the entire city is now a maze of dead ends, winding corridors, twists and turns. Officials are seeking the advice of expert Dr. Jean-Marc Croute, recently arrived from France, where he did extensive mathematical and scientific research involving the famous Labyrinth of Chartres Cathedral."

A helicopter view showed the city: *it looked like a maze made out of Einstein's head.* Chuck gasped. "Oh, my god!" He raced back to the phone to comfort his poor mother. She was crying.

"Oh, Chuck, what am I going to do? They're hoping to get us out of here on that helicopter, or maybe some other helicopters, but, honestly, they say the walls are into the clouds, and we're expecting another blizzard tonight! Oh, Chuck! And my head hurts, and my stomach—" She was wailing, crying, wailing.

"Mom, just stay warm. Are you warm, Mom?"

She sniffed. "Yes, sort of. The heat hasn't gone out in the office. Not yet, anyway."

"Is the dentist still there?"

"Well, of course he is, and the whole staff, too! Where else would we go? We're trapped in Einstein's head. *We're trapped in a Labyrinth of Doom!*"

Your Quest Journal:

1. Save the hockey team from Digger McGraw: **FAILURE.**
2. Find the secret of the tardigrades: **FAILURE.**
3. Go to the Ice Cap: **FAILURE.**
4. Find the Labyrinth of Doom: **FAILURE.**
5. Teach Melody some video-game basics: **SUCCESS.**
6. Learn how to control time: **FAILURE.**
7. Unlock the tenth level: **FAILURE.**
8. Get an escort to Greenland: **FAILURE.**

Your Inventory:

- Hockey stick
- Photos of hockey heroes
- Memory of the Tower of Darkness world
- Photo of Scott Metcalfe and the Demon of Runes
- Egyptian painting
- Candle in a wall holder
- Ankh
- Screws
- Most Manic award
- Fists of Fury award
- One club

- One wad of dynamite
- *Greenland's Underground Delights*, the textbook
- One broken wok

NHL 2001: GAME OVER. CONTINUE?

SSX SNOWBOARDING: GAME OVER. CONTINUE?

SUMMONER: GAME OVER. NEW GAME?

TIMESPLITTERS: GAME SAVED. CONTINUE?

THE BOUNCER: BEGIN NEW GAME?

Special Bonus! Chuck Farris Presents Hot TimeSplitters Tips

Here I am again, preaching to the choir about the wonders of video games. I think that tonight I'll have to beat TimeSplitters or Summoner, or some other game, just to see if the Demon of Runes is around to unleash my superhero powers again. Something tells me I'm going to need some superhero powers to fix things here in Poultrieville, to get the school back to normal, to turn the city back into a city from its Einstein's head construction, to keep the Darkness out of the world.

I don't know how I get mixed up in all this nonsense, really. I don't ask for these problems, you know. I get sucked into them because this Demon of Runes guy is hooked into the real-unreal world of video games, and he thinks I'm the best.

Well, let me make this quick, then, as I have a lot to do tonight, and there's still school waiting for me in the morning. Not to mention homework. I want to tell you a little bit about this terrific PlayStation2 game called TimeSplitters.

There are a bunch of ways you can play this game. I've done them all. In story mode, the bad bots and enemies are always in the same locations. If you beat the first three levels in easy mode, then you unlock the next three levels. After you beat the second three levels in easy mode, you unlock the last three levels. *There is no tenth level.*

Okay, so after you beat all nine levels in easy mode, you get to play the levels again in normal and hard modes. Melody is still stuck in easy mode somewhere in levels seven through nine.

There's also something called arcade mode, and something called challenge mode. If you finish all nine levels in challenge mode, then you unlock the cheats.

As you have probably guessed, there's a lot more to the modes than I just outlined. For example, arcade mode has all sorts of types: deathmatch, bagtag, capture the bag, knockout, escort, and last stand. These are specific kinds of games. In bagtag, your character carries a bag everywhere, trying to keep bad bots and enemies from taking it from you. In capture the bag, you try to get the opponent's bag and bring it back to your own base. In knockout, all the bags are in a central location, and you have to get them and bring them all to your base. *In escort, some guy on your team walks through the level like a zombie, and your job is to protect him until he gets to the finish.*

I'll tell you more about TimeSplitters later, I promise; but right now I want to pop Summoners into my PlayStation2, play all night until I beat it, try to regain my superhero powers, and maybe crash for a few hours before dragging off to school in the morning. Do they make you guys get up at 5 AM and start your first class at six-thirty in the morning? It takes me a whole hour to get down the highway in bad weather like this . . .

Hey, maybe I'll get lucky, and they'll cancel school tomorrow!

I hate peanut butter and jelly,

and I hope your dinner was better than mine—

Your pal,

Chuck Farris

3

DIGGER MCGRAW GOES NUTS AGAIN

Your New Quests:

- ☞ Solve the Einstein's head maze
- ☞ Find the center of the Schnooky maze

Chuck got very little sleep that night. By the time school rolled around at 6:30 AM, he was exhausted. Where was his mother? What was all this nonsense about Labyrinths of Doom and Einstein's head and dead-end Main Streets and Greenland? School didn't shut down for the day, as he'd hoped. Chuck made sure to wear his hat and gloves and his heaviest coat. He pulled on his boots and set off down the road toward the village. The highway was slick with ice, and the trees sagged from the weight.

Traffic was sparse. Perhaps one car slid past Chuck at one mile an hour. For a change, the highway was silent. The only sounds were the cracking of tree limbs from the ice, and the occasional caw of a terrified bird. There was no sound of water dripping; apparently, the ice wasn't going to melt anytime soon.

At school, Chuck twiddled with his combination and opened his locker. Chuck, Josh, and Melody all had lockers right outside Miss Olivia's social studies class. As Chuck shoved his brown bag into the mess on the bottom of his locker, Josh showed up, looking as if he'd just come home from a relaxing Caribbean cruise. Of course, Chuck hadn't a clue whether his friend had ever been on a cruise, much less to the Caribbean, and truth be known, Chuck didn't even know where the Caribbean was. But guys with lunches like Josh Samson's probably went on lavish vacations—it made sense, didn't it? Speaking of which, Chuck asked, "So what do you have for lunch today?"

Josh swung open his locker. It was neat and tidy, as usual: books on the carefully constructed solid mahogany shelf, sweater dangling on the blue plastic hanger, Game Boy on a stack of labeled textbooks and folders. Josh put his lunch on the mahogany shelf, where his father had hand-carved the phrase *Mom's Lunches* into the wood. "Nothing much. We had wings and pizza last night, so my mom packed me a bunch of that—"

Chuck's mouth started watering. He held the drool behind his teeth so it wouldn't drip all over the floor and onto his shoes.

"—and she made some nice spumoni ice cream with my grandma's cherries and mint leaves from last summer, too, so I have a cup of that for dessert."

Un-freaking-believable. Who else other than Josh Samson had ever even heard of homemade spumoni ice cream? And what other kid on the entire planet ever had pizza and wings for lunch, packed with his mother's six special sauces?

"What do you have?" asked Josh.

Chuck had his usual lunch, same thing he had for dinner last night: peanut butter and jelly on stale white bread, and one shrunken, rotting apple. "Nothing particularly fancy," said Chuck.

"Maybe I can share some of my wings and spumoni with you, huh?"

"That's only *one* of the reasons I call you my best friend, Josh," said Chuck, smiling. Now he had something good to think about all morning while the teachers droned on and on about math twisters and geography and grammar. He would think about *lunch.*

"Hey," said Josh, "remember that time when your mom packed you the frozen spaghetti in a bag?"

Chuck glared at him. "No, did she *really*?"

"Well, yeah, she did." For a smart guy, Josh could be a real dope. "Don't you remember? The sauce was still frozen solid—where there *was* sauce, that is." Josh was starting to laugh hysterically between the words.

Chuck just stood there, arms folded across his chest, listening to his friend. Let the guy have his fun—what harm was there in that? Chuck certainly couldn't defend his lunches. No way.

"Yeah yeah yeah, and the spaghetti part was all frozen, too, and mushy where it was thawing. It was so disgusting, Chuck, god, I thought I was gonna die just watching you crack it all against the lunch table."

Chuck started laughing, too; he couldn't help himself. His mother had tried to give him something different for a change. He'd been sitting there, pounding his frozen spaghetti in a bag against the side of the lunch table, trying desperately to whack off a few chunks because he was starving, when the lunch lady caught him and hauled him off to Mr. Calhoun. When the principal saw Chuck's lunch, he decided not to punish him. Instead, Mr. Calhoun gave Chuck free cafeteria lunches for a whole week.

Those were the good old days.

As Josh swung his locker shut, Chuck said, "Wait a minute, buddy. What's that?" He pointed to something on the Mom's Lunches shelf. It wasn't Toonsylvania, Chuck's favorite lunchtime game, and it wasn't a bundle of food. Rather, it was a pile of computer disks and what looked like hardware.

"I've been working on a little surprise for you, actually. I'm not very good at it yet."

"At what?" asked Chuck.

"At programming and video graphics. In fact, I suck."

Chuck shook his head. "I don't understand. Exactly what are you up to, and what's this got to do with me?"

Josh pulled the stuff from the Mom's Lunches shelf. "Come on, we have to go to class." He closed his locker and pushed Chuck toward Miss Olivia's room. "These are disks containing the code of my new PlayStation game, the one I've been working on forever, actually. Like I said, it sucks so far. This thing—" he waved a gray box with a one-foot cable tail on it "—is my PlayStation disk drive."

Cool. A way to make your own games? More than cool.

Josh shoved Chuck toward social studies class. Chuck's nose bumped into the door. He twisted the knob, then turned slightly. "So . . . ?"

"Yeah, well, I can save game data on ordinary floppy disks, and I can plug this thing into the memory-card slot, you see."

"But you don't have a PlayStation," Chuck whispered. "Your parents don't allow you to have video games in your house."

Josh nodded, anxious to get to class. The bell was going to ring. "I'm developing my game on my father's computer. I transfer the stuff to these disks. When you're sleeping, cramming sandwiches into your face for hours, or when you pass out from playing basketball, I use your console and test my stuff."

"What?"

"Yeah, it's no big deal. Now, come on!"

They went into Miss Olivia's social studies room, and Chuck immediately settled into his metal chair and sank his head onto his folded arms. He shut his eyes.

So his best friend was sneaking stints on his PlayStation while Chuck was wiped out. That was okay, no big deal. But what was Josh creating? Chuck couldn't wait to see the new game. There was no way it sucked, as Josh claimed. Josh was a genius. Any game he'd create had to be awesome.

Then Miss Olivia started chattering about next week's test, and Chuck's mind turned to other things, more dreamy, sleep-inducing thoughts . . .

Wings and pizza, wings and pizza. Meatball subs. Cream pies. Cap'n Crunch and cinnamon toast.

"Chuck Farris?" It was Miss Olivia's voice.

"Here." His head popped up, and he waved at the teacher.

"I wasn't calling roll, Mr. Farris," said the teacher. "I asked you to tell the class about Peter Freuchen. Do you remember yesterday's lessons?"

Chuck must have slept through social studies class yesterday. Why did they always schedule school to start at six-thirty in the morning?

"Um, Peter Freuchen," said Chuck, "he was, he was—" Chuck glanced at Josh, sitting next to him. Miss Olivia pretended that she didn't see him doing it. Josh mouthed the words: Greenland (mumble) 01.

Chuck said, "He was a guy in Greenland 101."

Miss Olivia graced him with a slight smile. She was old, even for a social studies teacher. Her hair was pure white and so frizzy it was like a halo. She wore bird glasses on the tip of her nose. They kept falling off, but the black chain around her neck let them drop to her chest instead of the floor. "Not quite," she said. "That would imply that Mr. Freuchen attended a college and took first-year Greenland class, which is ridiculous. Can anyone tell me something more about Mr. Freuchen? Josh?"

Josh practically fell out of his chair. He was always so thrilled to answer questions in class. On the other side of the room, Melody Shaw was chewing on her pencil eraser and whispering secrets to a girl sitting next to her. Melody smiled at Chuck, and he quickly looked back at the teacher.

Josh said, "It was in 1901 or so, and Peter Freuchen

was one of the first scientists to live for a long time in the worst region of Greenland. He studied medicine in Denmark; he ended up marrying and having children with an Inuit woman. He was an amazing man. He built a research station by the Ice Cap. And he lived there alone for really long periods."

This time, Miss Olivia's smile was much broader. "Excellent answer, Josh. The research station was actually a tiny wooden hut, and the weather was so cold that, as Freuchen simply breathed, his breath would condense and form so much ice on the walls that the hut grew smaller and smaller in size."

Josh and a few other brains laughed at the anecdote. Melody was writing notes to her friends and paying less attention to class than Chuck.

"There were wolves," said Miss Olivia, as she clomped across the room in her heels and flipped off the lights, "and these wolves ate Freuchen's dogs at night." She placed a slide on the overhead projector.

Chuck forced himself to stay awake, a next-to-impossible thing to do this early in the morning in a dark room with an elderly social studies teacher talking and showing overhead slides. On the other hand, she *was* talking about Greenland and the Ice Cap. This was important information. Maybe she'd even mention tardigrades.

The first slide showed a man standing in front of a sky-high mound of dirty ice. "Yes, class, this is the Ice Cap of our planet. Greenland itself is shaped like a tusk, and only the outer edges of Greenland support life such as grass and flowers. The entire inner portion of Greenland is ice. It's thickest up north, where Freuchen's little hut was located. In fact, the Ice Cap, which is actually a dome of ice, is two miles deep."

Chuck blinked at some slides of Greenland. One displayed the coastal valleys, where reindeer lived among bouquets of flowers. Chuck wouldn't mind living there. He pictured himself with a long beard and a name tag reading *Chuck Freuchen, Scientist*. Another slide showed some arctic foxes, alpine hares, and very prehistoric-looking musk oxen. There was a photo of a man walking across a vast surface of ice hills and caves, and another of a woman on a rope, dangling inside an ice chute.

"Cool," said some kid.

Or *freezing*, thought Chuck. He was mesmerized. Did the Demon of Runes live in chunks of ice somewhere in Greenland? Had he left the Tower of Darkness, which was his old home in the forest?

Miss Olivia looked like a specter, a ghost, on her little stool by the overhead projector. The light hit her glasses, but other than the lenses her face and body were dark outlines against the even darker blackboard.

She was heading into drill mode, where she acted like a military sergeant, pounding the class with questions that only Josh Samson could answer. "How much does the Ice Cap weigh?"

Josh: "Experts estimate 300 trillion tons."

Miss Olivia: "Yes, very good, Josh. What would happen if the Ice Cap popped off the planet?"

Josh: "The earth would bounce up like a sponge cake after you press it."

Miss Olivia chuckled. The class tittered, and some kids groaned. From the back, Digger McGraw hooted. Chuck's arm hairs rose, and a cold shiver shot down his neck.

"Hey, dudes, so maybe you can go snowboarding there in Greenland, huh? Say, teach, did this Fruitcaken guy ever go snowboarding on his ice caps?"

"No, Digger, I doubt it. He lived at the turn of the century, remember?"

Digger snorted. Chuck couldn't resist looking at the bully. All the kids were staring at Digger in the darkness. Melody had stopped whispering and passing notes. Even Josh had lost interest in the overhead slides.

"So," said Digger, rising to his feet and walking toward the front of the room, "there are all these ice caves up there, right?"

"That will be enough, Mr. McGraw. We've had enough trouble from you this year. Please return to your seat." Miss Olivia walked toward the light switch by the door.

"I don't think so, Miss Olive Oil, because I've got something to say to my pal over here, Chuckie the Fruit Fly Boy."

Chuck's mind went on red alert. He was no longer sleepy, no longer dreaming about cream pies or about being Chuck Freuchen. His body shifted back in his chair, and the chair almost toppled to the floor. He grabbed at the metal desktop, clutched it for balance, steadied the flimsy chair-desk.

"Yeah, Fruit Fly Boy," said Digger, "come and get some from ol' Digger McGraw. I wanna go snow-boarding again with you. I wanna go caving in the ice like old Fruitcaken did. Whaddya say, Video Boy, you up for some?"

Digger grabbed Chuck's T-shirt and wrenched him up from the chair-desk. Chuck's legs got caught beneath the desk contraption. His thighs banged against the underside of the metal desktop. He shoved the desk from his body, sending it flying toward another kid. Chuck hadn't meant to do that. His super-strength must be kicking in. He had to be more careful. The kid dodged the flying desk, leaping from his own seat to the floor and rolling to safety. Both desks crashed farther into the room, causing a spreading panic, as desks crashed in a rippling effect and flew against the back wall, knocking a shelf of *Geography of the World: The Eighth Grade* to the floor. A copy of *Greenland's Underground Delights* careened off the broken shelf and hit Chuck's head. *That was the name of the book that Melody's TimeSplitters character was reading.* Chuck had to get that book.

He staggered and clutched at Digger's body. Digger slapped his right cheek. Digger slapped him again, this time on the left cheek. Chuck growled and balled his fists.

Miss Olivia was in the hallway, shouting for help. Mr. Viking, the janitor, raced into the room, clutching a steel pail with a rag hanging out of it. He was wearing a construction worker's hard hat with a lamp on the front of it. "You again!" yelled the janitor, leaping at Digger McGraw. To Chuck's horror, he saw that Mr. Viking wasn't carrying a steel pail; rather, it was a can of Industrial Strength Bug-Off. It came in a canister the size of a milk jug. It had crossbones on the front. Chuck would know it anywhere. The Bug-Off rag flew into Josh's face, and Josh raced for the door, screaming, "Water, I need water! Someone get water! My eyes are burning!" Josh's glasses fell to the floor by the open doorway.

Chuck didn't have full superhero powers, *not yet*. He had purposely *not* beaten any video games since the Tower of Darkness. All he could do was shove Digger off him and race for the door. He grabbed the copy of *Greenland's Underground Delights* that lay by his feet. He heard Digger and Jack Fastolf laughing behind him, calling him names like Fruit Fly Boy and Little Pansy Video Baby. He heard his shoes crunch down on Josh's glasses, cringed as he realized he'd broken them, cringed yet more as he heard the bullies behind him as he raced after Josh. The janitor followed them all, whirling the Bug-Off canister over his head, spraying the walls and lockers with insecticide. And then the can was empty.

Chuck raced down the hall toward the stairs. But the stairs were no longer there. Instead, there was a giant gray wall that cracked through the ceiling into the sky. Chuck almost slammed into the wall. He thrust out his arms, and his palms crashed into the wall. The impact should have broken his hands off his wrists, but he barely felt anything: only a brief twinge of pain. He pushed off from the wall, then turned quickly and ran in the other direction. Digger and Jack followed him. He could feel their smelly, rotten breath on his neck. They were too close.

He careened around a corner, heading toward the front door of the school, the door right by Mr. Calhoun's office.

"Boys! Boys, what are you doing?" yelled the principal, dashing from his office, followed closely by the secretary.

Chuck raced for the front door.

There *was* no front door. It was another dead end, a gray wall sticking up into the sky. Behind him, Mr. Calhoun screamed. Papers were flying everywhere. Mr. Viking had given up. The janitor collapsed in the middle of the floor by his empty crossbones canister.

Digger slammed into the dead-end wall and fell backward onto the janitor. Jack Fastolf stopped short, barely missing a triple collision.

"Where's the door?" yelled Chuck.

"Over here," squeaked a voice.

Josh.

Chuck looked over his shoulder. Where Mr. Calhoun's office had been only moments ago, there now was a room lined with calico fur, with two breathing nostrils in the center.

Chuck raced into the office, found another exit, ran from it into a fur-lined hallway. From there, he ran until the hallway dead-ended and branched in two directions; following one path, and then another and another, Chuck ultimately came to the terrifying conclusion that Poultrieville Middle and Senior High School was now a maze, and that maze had a particular pattern: the school was a maze of Schnooky's head.

Your Quest Journal:

1. Save the hockey team from Digger McGraw: **FAIL-URE.**
2. Find the secret of the tardigrades: **FAILURE.**
3. Go to the Ice Cap: **FAILURE.**
4. Find the Labyrinth of Doom: **FAILURE.**
5. Teach Melody some video-game basics: **SUCCESS.**
6. Learn how to control time: **FAILURE.**
7. Unlock the tenth level: **FAILURE.**
8. Get an escort to Greenland: **FAILURE.**
9. Solve the Einstein's head maze: **FAILURE.**
10. Find the center of the Schnooky maze: **FAILURE.**

Your Inventory:

- Hockey stick
- Photos of hockey heroes
- Memory of the Tower of Darkness world
- Photo of Scott Metcalfe and the Demon of Runes
- Egyptian painting
- Candle in a wall holder
- Ankh
- Screws
- Most Manic award
- Fists of Fury award
- One club
- One wad of dynamite
- *Greenland's Underground Delights*, the textbook
- One broken wok
- Construction worker's hard hat with lamp

NHL 2001: GAME OVER. CONTINUE?

SSX SNOWBOARDING: GAME OVER. CONTINUE?

SUMMONER: GAME OVER. NEW GAME?

TIMESPLITTERS: GAME SAVED. CONTINUE?

THE BOUNCER: BEGIN NEW GAME?

Special Surprise Bonus! Chuck Farris Presents Weird Hockey Trivia and More NHL 2001 Tips

This is something new. I haven't done this before, but I thought it might be fun for a change. While I'm running through this maze of my cat's head, I'm thinking a million things, like:

Cap'n Crunch is my favorite cereal. It's also the nickname of a hockey player named Gilles Marotte of Los Angeles. I've always thought that was a funny name for a hockey player, and I bet the guy body-slams people really hard on the ice.

Remember the Zamboni, the machine that cleans the ice between periods? Well, I "pulled a Zamboni" the other day, when I fell down like a moron, scraping snow off the ice and lying there in a heap like a dead guy. That's called "pulling a Zamboni," and I'm still really ashamed of myself for falling down like that in front of Digger McGraw.

There was actually a hockey player named Batman. You know why? Well, it was in 1975 during a Stanley Cup final game between Philadelphia and Buffalo, and a bat was flying over the rink during the first period. Jim Lorentz, playing for the Sabres, killed the bat with his hockey stick. No kidding! And then some other guy, Rick MacLeish from Philly, scooped up the bat and stuck it into the penalty box. From then on, Jim Lorentz was known as Batman.

Some neat stuff about the NHL 2001 video game is (1) you can adjust the friction of the puck; (2) you can adjust how fast your team skates on the ice and how fast they get tired; and (3) you can choose and trade players, and create dream teams. You can play as a beginner, rookie, pro, or all-star. But be forewarned, in case your mother likes to yell at you to get off the PlayStation2 and go to bed: each hockey game lasts for an hour and a half or two hours. If you play real ice hockey, then you can always tell your mom that the video game helps you shoot goals on the real ice. If she's anything like my mom, she won't believe you, but at least you'll get her to laugh, and she might let you play for an extra half-hour!

How's that for a hot tip?

Chuck Farris

4

DOCTOR JEAN-MARC CROUTE UNLEASHES THE ULTIMATE LABYRINTHS OF DOOM

Your New Quests:

☞ Learn how to program complex mathematical mazes on the computer

☞ Solve the sliding-door maze to get out of the village

☞ Find Mary Croute

"Let me get this straight. You're telling me that the school turned into a maze of your cat's head?"

"Yes," said Chuck. He sipped some herbal tea. It was sweet, but not as cloying as grape jam. The tea helped warm him. He'd left the school without his coat, hat, gloves, or boots; there'd been no time to retrieve anything from his locker on his race to get out of the cat's head. "I swear it's all true, I swear," he said.

"Oh, I believe you, son," said George Croute's father, also known as Doctor Jean-Marc Croute, the man who had studied the Chartres labyrinth in France for years. It was a lucky thing the guy was George's father; and after Chuck finally found his way out of

Schnooky's head into the teacher's parking lot of the school, he had hightailed it to George's house, hoping to find the doctor "in."

They were in Doctor Croute's study, a book-lined room of vast proportions—this one room was at least the size of Chuck's entire house. Everywhere, the shelves displayed books about labyrinths: *The Health and Peace Labyrinth, Dowsing the World's Underground Channels*, *Your Inner Energy and the Labyrinth, Walking through Chartres, Earth Labyrinths*, *Knossos Labyrinth*, and many others.

"What's happening, Doctor? Do you have any ideas?" asked Chuck. He was beginning to feel warm. He was wearing one of George's old flannel shirts. It was two sizes too big for Chuck, but it was warm, and that was all that mattered.

It was only seven-thirty in the morning, and George's father was still in his bathrobe. Blue-striped flannel pajamas peeked from beneath his maroon robe. His slippers were also dark blue. He hadn't yet shaved, and his whiskers gave him a rough-and-ready look. George had inherited much from his father, at least in physical appearance: both were tall and beefy, and both were built like wrestling champions, though in the father's case it was more like a forty-something-year-old *retired* wrestling champion.

Doctor Croute had soft blue eyes, and he wore glasses. He wiped the lenses on his robe and walked past Chuck to a computer by the rear window. Chuck lifted his teacup and followed George's father, who said, "I have some vague notions, of course, as to why the school is a maze of your cat's head, but, frankly, I've never seen anything of this magnitude before. The entire perimeter of the city is sealed, and the freeways are beyond the limits of Einstein's hair. It's all very peculiar, and very fascinating." The computer booted up while the doctor talked.

Chuck looked out the window into the Croute family's beautiful village yard. It reminded him of Josh's backyard a block away. It was a large yard with a fence around it, and it had bushes and trees everywhere; with all the snow, Chuck couldn't determine whether the Croutes would have flowers this spring, but the previous owners of the place had grown masses of them.

"I plan to build a labyrinth back there," said Doctor Croute, smiling.

"From large bushes and juniper trees, something like that?" said Chuck.

"No, no, son, I'll simply mow the grass to form the circuit."

"I don't understand," said Chuck, sipping his herbal tea. He wondered if the doctor was a decent cook.

"You're not alone. Few people understand the labyrinth," said the doctor, as he clicked his mouse and entered information in some text boxes on his computer screen. A maze-generation program appeared on the screen. Some words displayed that told the user—in this case, Chuck—to enter the maze width and height, its wall and path colors, and various path dimensions. "This isn't a labyrinth, of course, but rather it's a maze."

"What's the difference?" asked Chuck. He set his cup on the desk. He had finished the tea, and while he wanted more, he was embarrassed to ask for it.

"A maze has dead ends, many paths and forks—choices—and it exercises the logical left side of your brain. A labyrinth, on the other hand, has only one circuit, one path, and it gives you no choices, no dead ends: just one carefully devised route into the center. The labyrinth exercises the creative right side of your brain."

Puzzling. So was the city a labyrinth of Einstein's head, or a maze of it? Was the school a labyrinth of Schnooky's head, or a maze of it? And was the Demon of Runes encased within a Labyrinth of Doom, as he claimed, or inside a Maze of Doom?

"The labyrinth I mow into my lawn next summer will have only one path, one beginning, and one end, Chuck. The point won't be to get lost in it. Rather, the point will be to enter at one place and to see clearly where you are at all times. The labyrinth should calm you, shed beauty upon you, and give you peace."

It sounded like hocus-pocus mumbo-jumbo to Chuck. All he knew was that his mother was trapped in a dentist's office in the middle of Einstein's head somewhere in the city, and she was sick and couldn't get out. It didn't sound particularly beautiful and peaceful. Nor was the school particularly at peace today. Digger was going nuts again, and with him the janitor, the principal, the teachers, and the kids. Right now, they were probably all running around the halls like maniacs, looking for a way out of Schnooky's head.

"Is the school a labyrinth, then? I found only one way out, or so I think."

Doctor Croute nodded. "It sounds like a labyrinth, Chuck, but one that's been formed by an unnatural event, same as Einstein's head downtown. Most labyrinths have calming effects on people, as I've said. These two particular labyrinths have disrupted everything. They seem to have been created by negative energy forces. As such, they may even be distorted into mazes."

Great. Why was Doctor Croute being so calm about all this? Chuck was nearly jumping out of his skin. He didn't want to see some silly maze-generation program on a computer. He wanted the school, the town, and the people to return to normal. How could a computer program do all that?

"I believe that someone stole my computer program a few days ago," said Doctor Croute, still calm, as if discussing the weather in an elevator. "It's my guess that someone is using this program to generate these bad-energy mazes, though how they're getting the mazes—or labyrinths—to generate in reality, rather than on computer screens, is beyond my comprehension."

Chuck stared past the bookshelves into the backyard. He wasn't sure what he was muttering, the words welled from a spring in his heart, but he heard the syllables roll from his tongue:

"coming from nowhere,
going nowhere,
deep within the leaves,

within the frost, the dew, the bark, the pear,
everywhere and nowhere,
all at once.
deep within the soil,
within the clouds,
reaching for nothing,
touching nothing,
and nothing touches it.
alone,
a single gem,
a jewel,
one drop that blazes the way to eternity.
—Spell of the peacock jewel"

And that's when the snow ceased to fall, and the sky suddenly blazed blue with a hot sun baking the ice from the fence. To the left, a black bear nuzzled its cub on a bed of green leaves. Overhead, birds buzzed past, dipping to avoid the crowns of the trees where winged peacocks sat in large nests of bear fur, waiting for the chance to catapult upon the smaller birds and feast.

Chuck turned, dizzy, and stared at the doctor, whose eyes were wide with astonishment. "I can't believe what I'm seeing," cried the doctor. "How did this happen?" He blinked rapidly, apparently trying to clear his vision, but the yard was warm, the sun was hot, and there were winged peacocks in large nests of bear fur.

"It's happening again, sir," said Chuck, sitting in the overstuffed chair in front of the computer screen. The doctor sat on the windowsill, his back to the scene beyond.

"What, Chuck? What is it? Tell me what this is all about, and maybe I can do something about it."

And so Chuck told George Croute's father everything he could remember about the Demon of Runes, about the Tower of Darkness, about Liu Bei and Xu Zhu from Dynasty Warriors, about Joseph and Flece from Summoner, about how he morphed into part Chuck Farris, part Xu Zhu, part Joseph, part Mac from SSX Snowboarding, and even part Paul Phoenix from Tekken Tag Tournament. Doctor Croute nodded his head, then stood and started pacing. What a relief that George's father believed him.

Doctor Croute paused in front of Chuck and said, "I'm still running the software on my computer, but someone broke in through this back window a few nights ago and stuck a zip disk into my drive and copied all of my algorithms and labyrinth files. It's taken me years to create these programs. In fact, Chuck, it's my life's work."

"But what does the code do, Doctor? And what does this have to do with the Demon of Runes and what's happening in your backyard right now?"

"My code generates complex mathematical labyrinths and mazes."

"Uh-huh. But they're just computer programs. How could they possibly make your backyard look like *that*—" Chuck stood and pointed out the window, forcing the doctor to turn and see it again, and the doctor winced and shielded his eyes, perhaps from the glare of the sun, perhaps from the realization that the world was going mad "—and how could they possibly open doors into the Darkness world, release the Demon of Runes, make everything into bizarre mazes all over the real world? *How?*"

Doctor Croute squinted at him. "Do you play chess, Chuck?"

"No, but my friend Josh Samson does."

"Then ask your friend Josh Samson how he analyzes the end point of any game."

"Say *what?*"

"The pieces are always in certain positions. Those positions vary. As in math, a good player can calculate his next move, and the moves after, based on the current positions of the pieces and their probable locations over the next X moves. Have you considered, Chuck, that certain events occur only when space and time align a certain way, and that space and time can be thought of as chess pieces in probable locations? Have you pondered that perhaps as space and time aligned to cause events, someone generated a labyrinth or maze, which opened up some very new and very strange possibilities?"

I come from the Tower of Darkness. Where it exists, I exist. The Tower of Darkness exists only when space and time align a certain way, when someone gains certain skills at a certain time. These were the words of the Demon of Runes.

"Do you have any idea what this means?" cried Chuck.

"No, I'm afraid not; I'm only suggesting possibilities that are beyond traditional proof."

"I need your help, and I need it immediately. I need

you to teach me everything you can—without all the mathematical mumbo-jumbo because I really suck at math—about these labyrinths and negative-energy mazes, and whatnot. I need you to teach me *now, right now*—"

"Can I eat my breakfast first?" asked Doctor Croute. "Can I shave?"

Chuck settled back into the overstuffed chair by the computer. "Don't you see there's no time for that?" he said. "You can't shave, and you can't eat. I believe it was Digger McGraw who stole your labyrinth code, Doctor, and I believe he ran it like the bozo he is on his computer at home, and he somehow accidentally generated a maze that opened the portal again into the Tower of Darkness world. He probably conquered a video game, he probably was high on Bug-Off or pasty blue flowers. He's like that, he'd even do it on purpose! The world's off balance, and I have to go home and conquer TimeSplitters, and I have to create a level of my own, a map of the ice tunnels in Greenland, a maze of the Ice Cap, and I must solve it totally, and I must regenerate whatever it was that Digger did on his computer, and I must return to the Tower of Darkness and save the Demon of Runes from that stupid bully!"

Doctor Croute put an arm across Chuck's shoulder, urged him from the chair. "Sit over here on the sofa by the kitchen door. I'm going to make us both some breakfast, Chuck. We're going to relax for half an hour, we're going to talk quietly and rationally about this mess, and then I'm going to help you fix it.

But for now, I want you to be calm, to sit down over here, and even to shut your eyes, if you want. You look exhausted."

Chuck did as George's father told him to do. But he didn't shut his eyes. He was wide-awake, much too alert and frightened to doze off.

Though . . .

The notion of breakfast cheered him up a little. His stomach was growling. He wondered what the Croutes ate for breakfast. Doughnuts? Pastries? Eggs and toast, maybe some bacon or pancakes?

"We can probably live without seeing any more of my backyard for now." Doctor Croute started closing the heavy curtains to block the view of the winged peacocks, bear nests, and blazing sun. But as the doctor pulled on the frayed gold cord, as he peered from the window one last time, he gasped. "Chuck! Come and see!"

Chuck hurried to the window. In the Croutes' backyard, where the lawn was bright green and abuzz with crickets and other insects, where birds dipped down to find spring worms in the dead of winter, there was now something else: the grass was mowed to form the whorls and turns of a giant maze that spelled the phrase CHUCK FARRIS, SAVE ME.

Doctor Croute looked as frantic as Chuck felt. "You're right, there's no time to eat, and there's no time to shave. I've never seen anything like this, and I don't know how to fix it. I fear the world's coming to an end. I'll teach you some of what I know, and I'll wish you luck. I don't know what else I can do."

Chuck couldn't take his eyes off the CHUCK FARRIS maze in the backyard. It was an elaborate maze, with very narrow corridors. It was one of the coolest things he'd ever seen—also one of the scariest. The end of the maze seemed to drop into nowhere. It disappeared into darkness as if culminating in a deep black hole.

The doctor eased Chuck back into the chair by the computer. "Just don't look at it," he said. "We have work to do if we stand any chance of solving the mystery of what's causing all these labyrinths and mazes to pop up out of nowhere. Here, just sit down and let me teach you a few things."

Chuck nodded, still dazed from the maze occupying the doctor's backyard. He didn't want to take his eyes off it—it was that bizarre—but he had work to do.

Doctor Croute showed Chuck how to generate mazes using his special algorithm. For what seemed like hours, Chuck sat there, entering numbers and colors in the text fields.

He generated a three-dimensional maze with long corridors and high walls. He solved it.

He generated a sliding-door maze, which required that he push balls and doors to move past obstacles. The sliding-door maze was easy for Chuck, as it was so similar to simple video games he'd played for years. He solved it.

He created mazes that looked like lions, Europe, and oceans. He solved them.

He created a triangular maze with one opening and one finish. He solved it.

He created a circular maze and solved it.

He created a complex maze in which each path had only one direction—that is, if he turned and tried to "walk" the other way on Doctor Croute's computer screen, the maze wouldn't let him continue. He created another maze that was so dense with corridors that he could barely see his way through them.

Without help from George's father, Chuck would not have been able to solve the more complex mazes. The doctor tried to show him the code, but Chuck didn't understand the odd symbols, stuff like "char* m,a,z,e=30,j[30],t[30]; main(c) {for *j=a=scanf(m= "%d",&c);" . . .

It was all way over Chuck's head. The doctor tried ramming more and more information into Chuck's brain: two-dimensional versus three-dimensional mazes, and mazes of higher dimensions; weave mazes, normal and planar mazes, orthogonal, delta, sigma, theta, zerta, and river mazes. There were so many types of mazes that it made Chuck's head swim.

Finally, Chuck gave up. "I'm going home," he told the doctor. "I have to find a way to the Ice Cap in Greenland. I have to find the Demon of Runes."

Doctor Croute nodded. "Look for negative-energy forces and let them guide you. Here, take this dowsing rod and let it show you the way." The doctor opened a closet door, retrieved a wooden pole with a ninety-degree angle in its center, and gave it to Chuck. "This will help you find the forces of energy beneath the earth. When it vibrates, you'll know that you're on a major energy source. Just remember: never operate out of fear, only out of courage."

Chuck was terrified about what he had to do. If he got lucky, he'd remain alive. Operate out of courage and not out of fear? Was there a difference?

George's father reached back into the closet and retrieved something else, and then added, "Take this coat, too. And these spare gloves and this scarf. Keep them for as long as you need them. We have plenty." He smiled warmly and urged Chuck to get home as quickly as possible before the storm hit harder and more havoc descended upon the village and the nearby city.

Chuck thanked George's father, and while he slid his arms into the coat and buttoned it, he said, "But, Doctor Croute, how will I know a positive-energy source from a negative one, and how will this dowsing rod help me find the Demon of Runes?"

"That I don't know, son." The doctor frowned. His fingers started playing with the buttons on his robe. "Listen, I'd come with you, but I have to wait here for George."

"I understand," said Chuck. It hadn't even occurred to Chuck to ask the doctor to accompany him home. "I've intruded enough upon you, sir. I know you have to help George, too."

Doctor Croute shut the closet door. It was heavy, possibly thick oak, and intricately carved with Indian designs from the mid-1800s. "George is all I have. He's a good boy. I'm very proud of him, and sometimes I think that I worry too much about him. It's not as if he's a fool or a weakling, of course. On the contrary, he's quite intelligent and has enormous physical strength. But he *is* all that I have, and after what happened to his mother, I worry a lot."

How bizarre that George's father worried about his son. For all Chuck's father cared, Chuck could be carried off by circus monkeys, be living in a cage in a zoo, or be axe-murdered in the gutter. Chuck's father wanted to believe that Chuck really loved him, but beyond that his father could care less about Chuck. His father was a selfish man.

Chuck pushed the lowest coat button into its hole and wrapped the scarf around his head. He'd be getting hot soon, and, besides, he had to get out of here, get home, and get cranking on TimeSplitters, Summoner, and all his other games. He had to make a maze that would get him into the Labyrinth of Doom. He had to beat Digger McGraw and Jack Fastolf before they caused more trouble.

His mother was sick and still trapped downtown. Candy Malone was probably terrified and freezing to death in her home on the hill over the swamp. Or maybe Candy was still trapped in the school. The thought of all those little kids trapped in the school scared Chuck. What would they eat? How would they stay warm? Sleep? He shuffled his feet a bit, edged toward the hallway leading to the front door. "Listen, sir, it's been very kind of you to help with the algorithms and this rod and everything."

"I understand, you have to go. If you run into my George, ask him to get home right away, would you? Or better yet, have him go home with you and help you—my son is very strong, Chuck, if you haven't noticed—"

"Yes, sir, of course I've noticed. Everyone knows that George is a terrific athlete. And a really nice guy, too."

Doctor Croute said, "Don't let anything happen to George, Chuck. Like I said, he's strong, but he *is* human. You may need him, but keep in mind that I need him, too."

Baffled, Chuck agreed and, not knowing what to do, took the man's hand and shook it. He felt silly. It was as if George's father was confiding in Chuck, and Chuck didn't know how to react. Adults rarely, if ever, treated Chuck as an equal, much less a confidant. What was Doctor Croute trying to tell him, and why wasn't Chuck getting it? Was Chuck *that* stupid?

"Do you know why we moved here from France?" An abrupt and very odd question.

"No, sir."

"George never told you?"

"No."

"You know of my work with the labyrinth at Chartres Cathedral?"

"Well, sort of . . ."

"Labyrinths are real, Chuck. I know. I've spent my life working with them. They're *real*." For such a quiet man, he was getting awfully excited, almost manic. His hands were shaking, as were his arms and head. His eyes, with deep, dark circles under them, were darting from one wall to the other, from the ceiling to the floor. If he wasn't a genius, he might be insane. Chuck had always heard that there was a fine line between the two: genius and insanity.

"It's okay, Doctor Croute, everything will be okay."

"No, it's not okay." The doctor's voice lowered. He clasped his hands, as if trying to control the tremors. "The Chartres Cathedral has a rose window on the front that's the same size as the labyrinth that's cut into the lawns outside the front door."

"Uh-huh . . ."

"The meander pattern, often seen in labyrinths, dates back to prehistoric times, maybe fifteen to eighteen thousand years BC, Chuck. Do you know how long ago that is?"

Chuck nodded. He placed his hand on the front door knob, started turning it. "Uh-huh . . ."

Doctor Croute grabbed Chuck's hand, moved close, and stared at Chuck with such intensity that Chuck lowered his eyes. "Doctor Croute. Please."

"Don't worry, I'm not insane, if that's what you're thinking." The doctor let out a staccato laugh, then trembled, then controlled himself again. "Not insane at all. It's just that I know the truth, and most people don't know it at all. There are Viking labyrinths, created by the same men who traveled the seas and swept through places like Iceland and Greenland. Yes, Chuck, it's true, and there's so much more I could tell you. But I must wait here for my George. He's all I have."

Chuck removed the doctor's hand from his own, and he said with as much compassion as he could muster, "Listen, Doctor Croute, you're worried about George and these oddball labyrinths popping up everywhere, and it's all understandable. Believe me, I'm plenty scared myself. You just told me that I'm supposed to operate out of courage, not out of fear, and you need to do the same. We need you, we need your knowledge, we need you to hold steady. I may have to go now, but I'll be back. You may hold the key that I need to find the Demon of Runes and conquer Digger McGraw." It was ridiculous that Chuck was trying to calm a world-renowned scientist. Why was he always thrust into the role of hero and protector? Why did he always feel like the *adult*?

I just want to be a kid.

"Go," said Doctor Croute, opening the door and gesturing for Chuck to leave his house. "Just be careful—use the dowsing rod."

A blast of wind gushed into the house from the open door. Ice shards were battering the wallpaper by the closet. Chuck began to shiver.

"My wife, George's mother, was killed in the labyrinth in front of Chartres Cathedral."

Chuck jumped and shut the door against the wind. "Say what?"

"Yes, it is so. She was a spiritual woman, a devotee of the dowsing rod and its ways. She felt the energy from the Genesa Crystals. She felt negative energies, Chuck. We went to Glastonbury Tor, a Gothic cathedral on the geomantic—that is, energy-producing—corridor in England. When the sun set one night, my Mary saw the negative energy glazing through darkness between the Gothic arches of the cathedral. She begged me to take her to Chartres, to the cathedral there, and so we went. She meditated within the

Chartres labyrinth. The sun was setting, as it had that night at Glastonbury Tor. I was in my study, trying to uncover the mathematical formulas leading to the negative energies within the English geomantic corridor. I heard a scream."

"Jean-Marc! Come quickly!"

The doctor raced from his study and to the front lawn of the cathedral.

"Jean-Marc, help, come quickly! It has me within its grasp! It won't let me go!"

The doctor entered the labyrinth, ran through its single corridor, made sure his boots did not infringe upon the grassy sides of the winding loops.

"I'm in the center! Hurry!" Her voice grew dim.

His mind flashed to the image of their infant son, George, asleep in the room by the study. Then his mind riveted again to the task at hand. George's mother. His wife!

"I'm coming! Hold still!" he cried, but there was no answer. There would never be another answer from his wife. For when he finally leapt into the middle of the labyrinth, the node in its very center, where the single loop brought him, she was no more.

Doctor Croute was crying. His head was bowed and resting in his hands. Chuck could see tears trickling between his fingers. "Doctor Croute, please, everything will be fine, I promise," Chuck said. He put his hands on the doctor's shoulders and squeezed a bit.

The doctor lifted his head again. "I'm sorry," he blubbered. "I'm so sorry. I lost control of myself there for a minute or two, didn't I?" He tried to laugh, but didn't quite pull it off. "You see, nearly sixteen years ago, my wife—and George's mother—disappeared inside a Labyrinth of Doom. She's probably dead. Ever since, I've devoted myself to understanding the negative energies. I hope to find her someday."

Chuck cleared his throat. He was afraid to ask, "So what brought you here, Doctor Croute—to Poultrieville, in particular? Was it—"

"Yes: the negative energies." The doctor slumped against the wall, sank his head into his hands again. "They were strong here. I felt it, my wife felt it. She's been gone so long. I wanted desperately to find her and bring her back—if not for me, then for my son. Take her dowsing rod, the very one she used at Chartres and at Glastonbury Tor. Find my wife, Chuck. Find George's mother."

Your Quest Journal:

1. Save the hockey team from Digger McGraw: **FAILURE.**
2. Find the secret of the tardigrades: **FAILURE.**
3. Go to the Ice Cap: **FAILURE.**
4. Find the Labyrinth of Doom: **FAILURE.**
5. Teach Melody some video-game basics: **SUCCESS.**
6. Learn how to control time: **FAILURE.**
7. Unlock the tenth level: **FAILURE.**
8. Get an escort to Greenland: **FAILURE.**
9. Solve the Einstein's head maze: **FAILURE.**
10. Find the center of the Schnooky maze: **SUCCESS.**
11. Learn how to program complex mathematical mazes on the computer: **SUCCESS.**

12. Solve the sliding-door maze to get out of the village: **FAILURE.**
13. Find Mary Croute: **FAILURE.**

Your Inventory:

- Hockey stick
- Photos of hockey heroes
- Memory of the Tower of Darkness world
- Photo of Scott Metcalfe and the Demon of Runes
- Egyptian painting
- Candle in a wall holder
- Ankh
- Screws
- Most Manic award
- Fists of Fury award
- One club
- One wad of dynamite
- *Greenland's Underground Delights*, the textbook
- One broken wok
- Construction worker's hard hat with lamp
- Disk of Doctor Croute's software
- One dowsing rod

NHL 2001: GAME OVER. NEW GAME?

SSX SNOWBOARDING: GAME OVER. CONTINUE?

SUMMONER: GAME SAVED. CONTINUE?

TIMESPLITTERS: GAME SAVED. CONTINUE?

THE BOUNCER: BEGIN NEW GAME?

5

WRESTLE MANIA! FENCE WITH THE DOWSING ROD!

Your New Quests:

- ☞ Fence Digger with the dowsing rod and win
- ☞ Force Jack Fastolf to stop selling beer to little kids
- ☞ Wrestle Digger McGraw and beat him with the Batman technique
- ☞ Find the Genesa Crystal, a.k.a. the peacock jewel

Chuck was stunned by Doctor Croute's request and half-believed that Mary Croute was encased within a Labyrinth of Doom. His head swirling with ideas—Viking labyrinths, prehistoric negative energies, and spooky old Gothic cathedral arches—Chuck staggered from the Croutes' house. It was hard to believe the doctor's story, yet Chuck himself had lived through worse: the Tower of Darkness, to name one example; the Demon of Runes, he reminded himself, unbelievable six months ago yet solid truth for the past two months; his own superhero powers. There was no reason *not* to believe Doctor Croute.

Chuck would do his best to find the Demon of Runes, to fix the world again, to find and save Mrs. Mary Croute, his friend's mother and the doctor's wife. *Geesh*, thought Chuck, *poor George never even knew his mother before she disappeared. At least my mother's alive.* Chuck couldn't imagine life without his mother.

He shoved his left hand deep inside his coat pocket, hurried through the snow, which was now up to his knees, toward the school. *I wonder what it's like to have a father like Doctor Croute. The guy's kind of cracked, but he sure loves his kid. Forget all that. I wonder what it's like to have a father at all.* His friend lived with only a father, while Chuck lived with only a mother. It was kind of weird. He'd have to ask George about it sometime.

For now, he was armed with some basic mathematical knowledge about labyrinth and maze algorithms, a disk of Doctor Croute's software, and a pole that detected energy inside the earth. It wasn't much to work with . . .

At Poultrieville Middle and Senior High School, kids were racing from the single opening out of the cat's head. The school no longer looked like a school. It no longer had walls, doors, and windows. The roof was either missing or so far into the sky that Chuck couldn't see it. He was standing by what appeared to be the cat's right ear. Kids were pouring out of the earlobe. The lobe was closing. Candy Malone squeezed from the tightening lobe, followed by several of her sixth-grade friends. Candy was scrawny and wore braces, and she was half Chuck's size. She dropped something in the snow. It was a bright pink jump rope. As Chuck ran closer, he saw his friends: Melody Shaw, Josh Samson, Vince Corelli, and George

Croute. Digger McGraw and Jack Fastolf were nowhere in sight.

Josh was panting. He dropped his hands to his knees and said, "I can't go on." His teeth were chattering, and his lips were blue. His glasses were filmed with ice like a windshield after a night storm. Chuck couldn't see his friend's eyes. And it was so cold outside that even tardigrades would have a hard time surviving in Poultrieville today.

"The glasses," said Chuck. "I thought I smashed them, Josh."

Josh nodded. "You did. These are my spares. They're three years old, and I don't see very well through them, but it beats no glasses at all."

"I'm really sorry, buddy," said Chuck. "I'll make sure you get a new pair, I swear. Can you see okay?"

Josh almost started crying. His face screwed into a terrible grimace as he shook his head no.

"Okay, give me the glasses. They're all fogged with ice anyway. I'll put them in my pocket, and you can stumble along with me. I'll help you." Chuck took his friend's glasses and slipped them into his coat pocket.

Chuck's friends weren't wearing their coats, but they all carried their backpacks with their books and other school stuff in them. "We had to escape quickly," said Melody through quivering blue lips. Her sweater was encrusted with ice, as were her hair, barrettes, eyelashes, and jeans.

Vince muttered an apology, then disappeared into a fog of snow and ice. He was heading to the apartment he shared with his mother and two brothers on the edge of the village. Chuck felt a twinge of shame for always feeling so sorry for himself. Vince had it so much worse than Chuck. Vince had to take care of his two younger brothers every day after school and on weekends, not to mention all summer and during the Christmas and Easter holidays. The poor guy was probably worried about his kid brothers, the two kindergarten twins.

George Croute pulled off his sweatshirt and handed it to Melody Shaw. "Hey, nice coat, Chuck," he yelled over the storm, gesturing at his own coat on Chuck's back. "Here, put this on," he said to Melody. She smiled her thanks and pulled on the heavy fleece sweatshirt, which was so large that it hung to her knees. "Now come on!" said George, pulling her by the hand and motioning to Chuck and Josh to follow him. He didn't give Chuck time to take off the coat and return it to him. Besides, as Chuck followed his friend's beefy body down the side road leading from school, he realized that he was wearing a really old coat of George's, that this coat would no longer fit George. Yet it was huge on Chuck.

They tramped down Pantella Path to Main Street. The rooftops wore thick white icing. Crystals continued to pelt them: Josh had his hands over his head to protect his face, and Chuck feared his friend was going to get sick by the time they reached Chuck's house; George looked cold but determined, with heavy white eyebrows—he kept blinking his eyes and shaking his head, and the snow fell like dandruff to his shoulders.

Chuck just forced himself to ignore the cold and the fear, and he kept moving down Main Street toward the highway. It suddenly occurred to Chuck that Josh didn't have to go home with him. "Josh, do you want to go to your own house?" he called over his shoulder. Josh could go to his own house and get warm more quickly and possibly avoid getting sick.

But Josh, true to his nature, shook his head; *No, he did not want to go home.* He stared at Chuck, as if saying, *I'm going with you to find the Demon of Runes. You're not doing this without me, no way.*

Where Main Street was supposed to feed into the single highway leading out of town, it ended at a looming wall of granite blocks. Chuck scowled, put his hands on his hips, turned toward his friends. George pointed down the road toward the main part of Poultrieville. The diner was gone, and with it the laundromat where Chuck got the family water on Sunday mornings. Also gone were the knife shop (*a front for the mob*, Chuck always thought—*I mean, whoever bought knives in Poultrieville, and for what purpose?*), the ostrich restaurant (long shut down for obvious reasons), and the barber shop. In their place was a giant wall, stretching high into the snow-dumping clouds.

They followed the wall, which was perpendicular to what used to be the commercial section of Main Street, until it forked into two corridors: left and right.

"We're in a maze." It was Melody, stating what they all knew.

"Can we go to my house instead of yours?" asked George. His long brown hair was thick with ice. He was shivering as much as Josh Samson now.

"No," said Chuck. "We need my video-game console and my video games. Besides, the only place we know of that the Demon of Runes visits here in the real world happens to be my living room."

"On Chuck's TV screen," added Josh.

Oh, brother. How were they going to make it out of town, down the highway, and to Chuck's house? "Come on," Chuck said, "we have no choice but to follow this labyrinth, or maze, or whatever it is, and figure out a way to exit from it."

He stumbled down the left corridor, his legs numb and stiff from cold. Then he hooked a right turn, then a left, then another left, and followed with a sharp right. Everywhere, he saw nothing but high granite walls. The houses were gone, the trees, the cars: everything about Poultrieville had somehow disappeared. Up ahead was a giant boulder, like some caveman relic, except this particular boulder had a huge, goofy smiley face on it. For crying out loud. What next?

"Come on, George, give me a hand." Chuck's teeth were chattering now, too, and it was hard to force the words from between his lips. George nodded, and the two boys heaved their bodies against the boulder. No luck—the giant rock wouldn't budge. "Again," said Chuck, and they both crouched, ran a few steps, and hurled their right shoulders against the boulder. A sharp pain flew down Chuck's arm, where Digger had speared him with the hockey stick.

"Oh, Chuck, be careful," said Melody. "Let us help."

"How can you help?" asked Chuck. Josh had no muscles, and Melody was a girl.

She glared at him. "Four people doubles what you have now, which is two."

But those two happened to be the strong ones, George Croute and Chuck Farris. Chuck glanced at George, who said, "No way, Melody."

Then George charged the boulder like a football quarterback. He even screamed like an attacking world wrestling champion. His body slammed into the boulder. He screamed in agony. The boulder moved forward half an inch.

Chuck hated smiley faces in general, and this one was blocking their way to safety. He remembered how the yellow heat had penetrated his body in the locker room. "Stand back," he said, "I'm going to try something." Perhaps he had some meager powers from his Tower of Darkness days. Perhaps the Demon of Runes had granted him some strength a little shy—to put it mildly—of superhero powers but a little stronger than average Chuck Farris powers.

He still had Doctor Croute's dowsing rod. He didn't know how to use the thing, so he stuck it in front of him and shut his eyes, trying to seek the negative energy.

Nothing happened.

"Hey, that's my mother's dowsing rod!" said George.

Chuck opened his eyes.

"Hey, what is that thing?" asked either Melody or Josh, or both of them together—Chuck couldn't tell.

"Yes, it was your mother's," he told George, "but your father gave it to me, hoping it would help us get to the bottom of the problems here, these very minor problems." He managed a weak smile, and George smiled weakly in return. "And this is called a dowsing rod, according to Doctor Croute," he explained briefly to Josh and Melody. "It's supposed to find the energy sources beneath the earth, something to do with energy flowing underground, all linked together, connecting everything, maybe causing upheavals and distortions in reality."

"Like these granite walls," added George, reaching for the dowsing rod. "Let me have it, Chuck. It was my mother's rod, and I used to play with it as a kid. My father taught me something about how to use these things."

"What are you talking about?" asked Melody, moving closer to stare at the rod. "What is this thing, exactly?"

George muttered some stuff that his father had taught him years before. "My dad says that labyrinths, and maybe some mazes, are a cosmic part of all the energy in the universe, that the spirals and corridors somehow are connected to underground energy and water lines beneath the planet's surface. Yeah, no kidding, and, hey, don't laugh at it, Josh, my mother disappeared in one of these things, these labyrinths, and may still be trapped inside it."

"I wasn't laughing," said Josh. He looked more frightened than anything else, and, besides, Chuck knew him well. Josh would never laugh at anything this scary. He was probably trembling from cold, and his lips turned a certain way; or maybe George was just really touchy about his father's weird occupation and the mysterious disappearance of his mother long ago.

"Yeah, well, don't laugh," continued George. "My father is a world expert in this stuff. So was my mother, in her own way. They both believed that the labyrinth spirals are linked to infinite movements of the planets, that the round forms of the spirals are feminine, that the balance of the labyrinths rely on intricate mathematics, that the asymmetry in mazes and some labyrinths helps the world grow, that certain crystals help promote the potency of these energies, whether positive or negative. Sorry," he concluded, "I know that I sound like a textbook. I've listened to my father since I was a baby." He grinned. Then he extended his arm, the one with the dowsing rod, and he concentrated. "Gateway of potentials," he said over and over again until Melody started giggling.

"This is like playing Ouija board or having a séance," she said.

"Quiet, Melody," said Chuck. "Go on. Do it again, George."

Melody and Josh turned away from Chuck and George. They leaned against the high granite wall. They were trying really hard not to laugh. Though Chuck still believed that Josh didn't have it in him to laugh at anything quite this serious. "For crying out loud, would you two try to stifle it a little?" he said.

"Sorry, Chuck," said Josh. "I'm not laughing, I

swear. I think the tension's starting to get to me, that's all."

"Yeah, me, too," said Melody, but she was giggling.

"Well, get serious. If you had seen George's backyard earlier this morning—I swear that was one scary place. It was all sunny with winged peacocks and weird labyrinths spelling my name. Hey, wait a minute! Hold out that rod again, George." When George shut his eyes again, pointing the dowsing rod down the corridor toward the giant boulder, Chuck reached his hands up toward the top of the labyrinth walls and chanted the magic words:

"coming from nowhere,
going nowhere,
deep within the leaves,
within the frost, the dew, the bark, the pear,
everywhere and nowhere,
all at once.
deep within the soil,
within the clouds,
reaching for nothing,
touching nothing,
and nothing touches it.
alone,
a single gem,
a jewel,
one drop that blazes the way to eternity."

A series of images flashed before his eyes: pyramids, shrines, cathedrals, stone circles; and he saw lines beneath the snow and the hard earth, lines of major power, all connected and crisscrossed, with all the power surging through them like some major electricity grid pumping out of Niagara Falls. And that's when the path was clear to him: and he saw the Schnooky's head labyrinth in the center of town, where the school used to stand; he saw what surrounded the Schnooky's head labyrinth: a fairly simple sliding-door maze.

At the school: the walls were made of bone and covered in dark calico fur; there were glowing green eyes, two of them, where Mr. Calhoun's office used to be; there were whiskers on the playground; the entrance was the left ear, the exit was the right ear. And while the whole thing twisted from corridor to corridor, from whisker to nostril to eyeball to lips to nose to ear, there was only one valid path through the cat head. In a moment of crystal clarity, Chuck saw the whole maze.

He also saw kids huddled in the ears, warming their hands in front of the glowing green eyeballs. He saw kids crammed against the fur walls, curled up and crying down by the lips and teeth. But he didn't see Digger McGraw or Jack Fastolf anywhere.

And that's when Chuck Farris realized he had once again turned into a video-game superhero, this time Captain Ash from TimeSplitters. He could see the mazes, the objects in them. He could see through time and space, to the earth below, to the sky beyond.

It was happening again.

"What's the matter with you?" George Croute was shaking Chuck by the shoulders. "Wake up, dude!"

"Yeah, yeah, I'm awake." Chuck peered down the corridor. The boulder was gone.

Josh said, "It rolled down the granite hallway there, Chuck, and disappeared after knocking into a wall and rolling to the left."

If the boulder had rolled elsewhere, then according to Doctor Croute's theory of sliding-door mazes, a door to the exit had opened somewhere else in the corridors. "We have to run!" Chuck cried to his friends. "Before the exit closes, we have to find it and get out of here!"

They dashed down the corridor, following the trail left behind by the rolling boulder. Chuck was leading, followed by Josh and then Melody, with George taking up the rear. *Power in the front and back*, thought Chuck; *safer for everybody that way. My god, I hope nothing happens to Melody and Josh. Why do I always have to get them mixed up in this junk?*

"Chuck!" screamed Melody.

Something large and soft fell from the sky and landed on top of Chuck, knocking him to the ground. He rolled over and saw a giant bat flying toward—

Digger McGraw!

The bat was at least the size of Schnooky, and its wings were larger than Chuck's feet. Digger had fallen with the thing, and now Digger pulled something from a hidden inventory—it was his hockey stick—and smacked the bat in midair. The bat swooped toward Chuck again. Chuck leapt up and pulled his own hockey stick from inventory.

Then something else fell from the sky, knocking George Croute to the ground. For a moment, Chuck's attention was diverted, and both Digger and the bat lunged, knocking Chuck back down. Chuck tried to beat Digger and the bat off his chest. He scrabbled to get back to his feet, but Digger was on top of him, pinning him to the cold ground. Digger smelled awful, like rotting meat, and he had those oozing pimples and greasy hair and chipped teeth and a wisp of a moustache—

"Digger McGraw! Get off of me!"

The chipped teeth formed a grin. "You called?" Digger raised his right fist.

From overhead, metal flashed—

A sword? What—?

And then George leapt to view, clutching his mother's dowsing rod, pointing it straight at Digger McGraw's cheek. "Get off him," said George.

"And what are you going to do with that pansy stick, huh?" sneered Digger, jumping off Chuck but keeping one foot on Chuck's chest, pinning him to the snow.

Jack Fastolf was there, too. He'd apparently dropped from the top of the wall with Digger. Jack pinned Melody to the wall. She started crying and hollering at him, trying to beat the shaggy blond lion-oaf off her back. Her face was pressed hard to the granite, and Chuck saw blood dribbling down her left cheek to her lips. It spilled over to her chin. Jack was laughing. He grabbed her wrists and pinned her arms behind her back. With a flash of terror, Chuck remembered all the rumors about Jack: that he sold beer to little kids—and worse even, that Digger sold cigarettes and drugs to kids. What would stop the two from forcing drugs on Melody Shaw, knocking her out, dragging her off somewhere?

Chuck's eyes saw white lightning, he lost all vision of reality for a second, and then, before he knew it, his hurt right arm lashed out, and his fist grabbed Digger's ankle and twisted, and then, with superhuman speed, Chuck was on his feet, shoving Digger to the wall, then releasing the bully and springing off the wall, back-flipping high into the air and coming down hard on top of Jack Fastolf. He knocked Jack off Melody and to the ground, and then he dove on top of Jack, rolling with him in the snow, scrambling to pin the bully down. Melody was still crying. She hurried over to Josh, and the two of them raced down the corridor toward the fork where the boulder had rolled. George Croute screamed, "En garde, sucker!" and he leapt at Digger again, but Digger had his hockey stick.

Jack's breath was on Chuck's face. The guy reeked of cigarette smoke. Chuck almost choked from the smell. Chuck wanted to punch him out, and he knew he could because he could feel his giant arm muscles hardening, and there was no pain where Digger's hockey stick had hit him that morning. Chuck had his burgeoning superhero powers back, but he resisted the urge to clobber Jack. Instead, he pulled Jack's stupid blond beard-thing and leapt to his feet and raced toward Digger, who was waving his hockey stick at George.

Something hit Chuck's face. It was big, furry, and nasty-looking. It was the bat. Chuck felt heat on his cheek and realized he was bleeding from where the bat clawed his face. With both hands, Chuck grasped his hockey stick and raised it high over his right shoulder. He let the bat have it: right in the belly! The bat screeched and slammed against the wall and fell to the ground. Chuck remembered Jim Lorentz, a.k.a. Batman, who had played for the Buffalo Sabres. He remembered reading about the 1975 Stanley Cup final game between Philadelphia and Buffalo, when a bat was flying over the rink during the first period. Jim Lorentz had clobbered the bat with his hockey stick.

And today, Chuck Farris had done the same.

Chuck stood back, keeping an eye on Jack Fastolf. The two of them watched for a minute in stunned silence, as Digger McGraw with his hockey stick and George Croute with his mother's dowsing rod . . . started fencing.

George ducked, pulled back his dowsing rod, and lunged at Digger, who held up his hockey stick, blocking the blow. The hockey stick swept to the right, then back, and then shot straight out, almost skewering George in the stomach. George shifted to the right, then thrust the dowsing rod at Digger again, getting the bully in the shoulder. Point, thrust, *lunge*. Digger winced slightly and laughed. "You can't hurt me, you idiot," said Digger.

And then George did a bunch of complicated maneuvers, yelling French words like "Coulé-dégage! Double coupe! Attaque dessous!" The dowsing rod was a forked sort of thing, so George was jumping around like a maniac, trying to get in position, duck hockey-stick thrusts, and jab Digger. Fake, parry, thrust, *lunge*. The bully raised his hockey stick and sent it crashing down toward George's scalp. Chuck shot forward, and his body collided with Digger's, and the bully went flying against the granite wall. His hockey stick flew into the air, hit the wall way up high, and came streaking back down, slamming into some ice farther down the path.

"Come on!" yelled Chuck to George, and they raced down the corridor, past Digger's hockey stick and around the bend, where the boulder had gone, followed by their friends, Josh and Melody.

They jumped over a short red fence that seemed to have slid down from slots on either side of the path. They darted around a half-open yellow door, they streaked past a green-marbled block of wood and a crate made of steel, over a metal horse, a rock cow, and a plaster chicken. This was one freaking weird place. They almost slammed into a wall that suddenly shot up in front of them, but managed to duck around it in the nick of time. It sealed the corridor behind them, preventing the two bullies from following them any farther. Up ahead, a crumbling house stood on a hill over a frozen swamp. It was the highway, and they were almost home.

Your Quest Journal:

1. Save the hockey team from Digger McGraw: FAILURE.
2. Find the secret of the tardigrades: FAILURE.
3. Go to the Ice Cap: FAILURE.
4. Find the Labyrinth of Doom: FAILURE.

5. Teach Melody some video-game basics: **SUCCESS**.
6. Learn how to control time: **FAILURE**.
7. Unlock the tenth level: **FAILURE**.
8. Get an escort to Greenland: **FAILURE**.
9. Solve the Einstein's head maze: **FAILURE**.
10. Find the center of the Schnooky maze: **SUCCESS**.
11. Learn how to program complex mathematical mazes on the computer: **SUCCESS**.
12. Solve the sliding-door maze to get out of the village: **SUCCESS**.
13. Find Mary Croute: **FAILURE**.
14. Fence Digger with a dowsing rod and win: **SUCCESS**.
15. Force Jack Fastolf to stop selling beer to little kids: **FAILURE**.
16. Wrestle Digger McGraw and beat him with the Batman technique: **SUCCESS**.
17. Find the Genesa Crystal, a.k.a. the peacock jewel: **FAILURE**.

Your Inventory:

- Hockey stick
- Photos of hockey heroes
- Memory of the Tower of Darkness world
- Photo of Scott Metcalfe and the Demon of Runes
- Egyptian painting
- Candle in a wall holder
- Ankh
- Screws
- Most Manic award
- Fists of Fury award
- One club

- One wad of dynamite
- *Greenland's Underground Delights*, the textbook
- One broken wok
- Construction worker's hard hat with lamp
- Disk of Doctor Croute's software
- One dowsing rod
- Bright pink jump rope

NHL 2001: GAME OVER. NEW GAME?

SSX SNOWBOARDING: GAME OVER. CONTINUE?

SUMMONER: GAME SAVED. CONTINUE?

TIMESPLITTERS: GAME SAVED. CONTINUE?

THE BOUNCER: GAME OVER. CONTINUE?

Special Surprise Bonus! Chuck Farris Presents Summoner Tips and Weird Fencing Trivia

You guys probably remember how hooked I was on the Summoner game a couple of months ago. Well, here I am, trudging down the highway with my friends, wondering why Digger McGraw had that weird fencing match with George Croute. I already know that my superhero powers are starting to come back. I'm able to solve complex mazes and race around granite walls and jump over obstacles, much as my favorite characters do these things in the TimeSplitters game.

I'm beginning to wonder if my Summoner powers are returning, too. Maybe that's why Digger and George got into that fencing match back in the Poultrieville sliding-door maze. Maybe the Demon of Runes is casting all these weird powers on me again, and just as it happened before, the weirdness is rubbing off on my friends. After all, Joseph in Summoner is a mighty good fencer.

So, with that in mind, here are some Summoner tips for you and some weird bits of fencing trivia. What else am I going to think about while I'm slogging my way down the highway over ice?

Summoner Tips: Getting Money

Money is scarce in the first part of the game. You can get money by completing quests and stuff. In the first half of the game, two thousand gold pieces may seem like a lot of money. Trust me, it's not. Two thousand gold pieces won't buy anything! By the way, I am exaggerating a bit. Two thousand gold pieces won't buy anything *good.* It might buy a long sword and two leather jerkins. Who cares?

Near the end of the game, you should have two pairs of midnight platemail. Since you have two, sell *both* of them. You might be wondering why I'm saying this, but *you don't need either of them!* Each sells for approximately 519,999 gold pieces. Also sell the horseman's platemail after you get the warrior's platemail. Horseman's platemail sells for the same amount as midnight platemail.

If you complete the Hunting Horn of Vadaghar quest, sell the nobleman's platemail. A chainmail tunic plus chainmail leggings equals 50 protection. So why put on something like midnight platemail that offers 50 protection when you can sell it for approximately 519,999 gold pieces? Platemail covers both the upper body and legs. After I defeated Luminar, I had 4,038,716 gold pieces.

Summoner Tips: Getting Experience

This one is obvious. Defeat monsters. Also, you might want to do the King of Talas, Haenul, and Gemstone of Eraekor quests. You can get about 50,000 experience points from the King of Talas quest, and about 30,000 experience points from the Haenul quest. Also note that you can obtain 100,000 experience points from the Durgan and Dakhanim quests . . . ☺

There's the smiley-face guy. Yeah, you guessed it: that's the way the boulder looked in the Poultrieville sliding-door maze.

Weird Fencing Trivia

Okay, I promised you guys that I'd give you some trivia tidbits about the sport of fencing. I've frankly never studied fencing in school, in the cornfields behind my house on the highway, in the dump, or in the Caverns of Luray—which I think are in Virginia, but I've never been to Virginia, you see; and I just like the sound of the Caverns of Luray, and this is my book, so I'm able to stick the phrase *Caverns of Luray* here in this section, hidden in the Weird Fencing Trivia.

That was a mouthful.

Here are some little quizzes about fencing trivia. These are really easy, and they may even be kind of fun. The answers are at the end.

1. What is a feint?
   - A. When Melody Shaw or Josh Samson collapses in a heap from fear.
   - B. A whiff of bad perfume worn by Miss Olivia on a hot day.
   - C. A false attack to fool your opponent.
   - D. How someone with a really poor command of the English language says "is not," as in this example spoken by Buddy Terwillogee in 1948: "Well, if it feint my old friend Joe. How ye doin', bud?"

2. What is a compound attack?
   - A. Same kind of thing as a chain attack.
   - B. A series of fencing attacks and maneuvers.
   - C. When bad guys or foreign agents bomb the presidential fortress home.
   - D. All of the above.

3. What was a major way of resolving disputes in the sixteenth and seventeenth centuries?
   - A. Mud fights
   - B. Duels (or fencing)
   - C. Axe smashing
   - D. Saber-toothed tiger races

4. What is an appel?
   - A. What I get for lunch every day with my soggy peanut butter and jelly sandwich.
   - B. When a guy deflects his opponent's sword.
   - C. A dramatic method of falling forward while attacking an opponent; also known as a flèche.
   - D. When a guy slams the floor with his foot.

5. Finally, what is plaque?
   - A. The junk on your teeth that the dentist removes.
   - B. The award a teacher gives you for doing really well in science or gym class.
   - C. The condition where the point of your sword is sideways and flat when it hits the opponent.
   - D. The condition where you angle around the opponent's blade and then strike.

Answers

1: C.

2: D.

3: B.

4: D.

5: C.

That's it for now. We're nearing my house, so I gotta go.

Chuck Farris

6

VENGEANCE IS THE KEY

Your New Quests:

☞ Find the secret of the red shoes

☞ Beat all the games to get the superhero powers

While his friends booted up the PlayStation2, Chuck dug through the closet by the front door for his father's old snowboard. That's where Chuck had put it in December after snowboarding against Digger in the fields across from The Dump, the name he and his mother used to describe their house in the country.

There it was: the worn red snowboard. Tears burned Chuck's eyes. Just seeing the snowboard hurt him. Memories welled, and he tried to force them back down into his brain. He hoped his friends would stay in the living room and kitchen for a few more minutes so he could indulge himself, remember better times when he was five and six, before his father left them forever.

Even heroes had to cry.

Even superheroes . . .

And Chuck was no hero. Everyone treated him as if he could save the world all the time, but they never seemed to understand how hard it was for him to step up to the plate and keep hitting those home runs. He was tired of being the hero. He wanted somebody else to be the good guy, to comfort Josh, to say the right things, to put Digger in his place, to save Melody from Jack Fastolf.

He peered over the waist-high, fake-wood banister separating the entryway from the living room. George Croute was handing Josh a cup of laundromat water. The cup was chipped at the top, like most of the cups in Chuck's house. For a second, shame burned through Chuck, but then he shrugged it off. He and his mother did pretty well, considering what they had to work with and how hard they struggled just to stay afloat.

What did his friends really think of him? Did George think Chuck was a jerk because Chuck and his mom were kind of poor and lived in The Dump with the laundromat water? Did Josh sneer about how dumb Chuck was behind Chuck's back? And Melody Shaw: did she want George Croute instead of Chuck because George was older, stronger, and lived in a cool house in the village with his really cool dad?

Chuck wished he could stop being the hero, just for once. Just for once he wanted to be plain old Chuck Farris, dope and lazy moron, slip-sliding through school, shooting baskets, running like he was gonna die if he didn't push any harder, just to push harder, just to push . . .

To make it through . . . something. Chuck never could figure out what he was trying to push through or where he was trying to get while he was pushing himself.

"I won't get old and die now, I won't live as if I'm gone: the angels swiped my red shoes and left me with a goodbye song." The tune would course through Chuck's brain while he ran, while he shot pucks, while he pushed himself to the limit and then some. It was an old Junk Cantrelle tune his father always sang when playing hockey with Chuck or snowboarding at the village park.

As he skated onto the ice, his dad would pull on his worn black work gloves, hiding the long scar on his right thumb, where an electric saw had sliced him right beneath the nail. Chuck liked that scar, and thought it was very macho. His mother had tried to get his father to take a job that wasn't as dangerous, but his father never listened to or cared about anything Chuck's mother said. So the scar fascinated Chuck. It was a symbol of machismo, yet it was also a symbol of his father's hatred toward his mother and his father's overall idiocy about the things that mattered in life, like his family.

"I won't get old and die now, I won't live as if I'm gone: the angels swiped my red shoes and left me with a goodbye song." What did it mean? Chuck didn't have a clue. Maybe his father left because he felt really old and like he wasn't having any fun, or maybe his father was tired of working so hard and living here in The Dump with Chuck and his mom. Or maybe, was it possible? . . . maybe Chuck's dad was just tired of living or something, of being the man, maybe he wanted the angels to swipe his red shoes, the snowshoes and everything around them, everything here in this house, or maybe the angels had already taken his red shoes, his happiness . . .

In the living room, the PlayStation2 was cranked, and Josh was pushing The Bouncer game into the console. Nobody called for Chuck. Nobody wondered what was taking him so long.

Did they care? Why did they bother to hang out with Chuck at all? Why?

He remembered his father's left foot in the forward position on the board. His father's giant foot with its gigantic toes. Dad's clippers were as big as tree trimmers, and the two blades would whack into his thick toenails as if sawing through giant tree branches. Everything about his dad was big. Dad had a big face and a big grin and a big laugh.

I love you, Dad. Why don't you love me enough to come here and take care of me and Mom? Why don't you love Mom? Why is it more important for you to be with your girlfriend, the store-clerk bimbo? Why is it more important for you to have lots of fun and no responsibilities? That's what I'm supposed to have—lots of fun and few responsibilities. I'm the kid, not you, Dad. I don't want your responsibilities. Why did you force them on me? I was only six!

Chuck stooped and fingered the snowboard where the foot straps were sticking up, all cracked and peeling from years of being stored in the basement, from years of overuse in the time before Dad left.

He was on the floor by the front door, sitting cross-legged now with his head stuck into the closet, his fingers fondling the old board.

Chuck swerved on the ice and slammed into the flimsy goal post in Harold Park.

"What are you doin', bud?" His dad always called him bud, like maybe Chuck was one of those fizzy beer drinks on TV.

Chuck was six. He tripped over his skates, and the ice slammed into his face. Blood was dripping from his face and freezing to the pond surface. Chuck pulled his face from the ice. "Daddy, I hurt."

His father laughed. He skated away from Chuck, his stick making big swirls and half-circles on the ice. "I won't get old and die now, I won't live as if I'm gone: the angels swiped my red shoes and left me with a goodbye song."

"Daddy?" It hurt to try to get up. Chuck grasped his stick in his right hand and pushed himself up on his right elbow. A spear of pain hit him, right in the chest, and he fell back to the ice.

Why did everyone always ignore Chuck when he was in pain? Why didn't they come and help him? Didn't he help everybody a lot like his mommy taught him to do? Why did his daddy always sing about stupid old red shoes?

It was dark outside, the time of night when his daddy always took him to the park to play ice hockey. There were no lights here in the park, only the dim throb of some street lamps beyond the church.

"He wants his red shoes, and he wants all the giggles, and he simply can't refuse." Daddy skated toward him, still singing. "What's the matter, bud? Come on, I'll help you up. Come on, let's play. I want

to play, Chuckie. Do you understand? Your father wants to play."

It was the last time Chuck ever played ice hockey with his father. Three days later, his father was gone forever. Maybe once a year, Chuck got a letter from him. He was happy with his bimbo store clerk, Dad wrote. He had a great job down south, he made lots of money, he had fun vacations. Chuck would cry and throw out the once-a-year notes. They made him sick.

He wanted to get even. He didn't know how, and truth be known, he didn't have the guts or any true desire to get even. It hurt. That's all. It just hurt. And he was angry.

"Chuck? What are you doing? You coming over here to play with us, or what?" It was Melody. She was calling to him from the living room.

Chuck bobbed his head over the banister, half-lifting himself from the floor. He forced himself to smile. "Sure," he said, "in a minute. I'm pulling some stuff out of the closet that I might need later."

"Okay, Chuck. Do you need any help?" Melody twisted from her position in front of the PlayStation2, where Chuck's friends were still playing The Bouncer. She started to rise, as if to come and help him.

"No," he said quickly. "I'm fine, it's no big deal."

She smiled briefly and returned to the video game.

Chuck wished they would all go home. He wanted to crawl into bed under his covers and cry.

"Vengeance is the key. If you're happy, let it be." That was another line from his father's old song, the Junk Cantrelle tune. What vengeance? Did his father want to get even with his mother? Did his father have any clue how badly he'd hurt Chuck's mother? Did his father even care?

No, no, and another no. His father had left because he wanted to have fun, he wanted to wear his red shoes and dance or something, he wanted his bimbo store clerk, he wanted to go on his vacations: he didn't want the responsibility of Chuck and his mother.

Chuck hated him.

Chuck wished he could see him.

Chuck wished he'd come back.

Chuck hated him.

"Chuck, what are you doing on the floor?" Melody draped an arm across his shoulder. She smelled like soap, and her face was calm and sweet, and she looked concerned. "I've never seen you like this, Chuck. I know you get quiet sometimes, but—"

That's when I go inside my house and leave you to play soccer alone in the field, Melody, he thought. *But you guys are inside The Dump now, and there's no place for me to go to be alone. You're all going to see me as I really am.* The thought terrified him. He couldn't bear for his friends to see him suffering, to see his weakness. They'd make fun of him for years, he'd lose his edge against the kids in sports, they'd all know him for what he really was: a weakling.

Melody's eyes were soft and brown. She lowered her voice to a whisper. "I know it's hard, Chuck," she said, and then "No, just stay and play The Bouncer, we'll be there in a minute," and Chuck bolted upright, realizing that Melody had just shooed George and

Josh back into the living room. Had they been coming out here to find him weeping like a moron on the floor by the closet?

Melody tugged him up by the elbow and took him down the hall into the bathroom, where she forced him to wash his face. He felt dopey. She was acting too much like his mother. On the other hand, he was relieved to push his father out of his mind and to forget again. He hated remembering his father and what had happened to his family. It was much easier to pretend that painful things didn't exist.

Maybe his father didn't exist.

Maybe his memories were just dreams. Maybe a red angel came to Chuck at night and gave him these awful memories, these endless nightmares.

"I'm okay," he said to Melody. He wiped his face on his mother's green hand towel.

"Your mother sure likes green a lot, huh?" said Melody.

He managed a laugh. "Red shoes. Green house. Story of my life."

"Red shoes?"

"Long story, Mel."

"Mel?"

"My new name for you."

"One of the guys, huh?"

"Something like that—"

She frowned.

"—but not quite a guy," he added.

"Come on, Chuck. Life sucks, I know it, we all know it. Look at George out there. His mother died when he was a baby, and his father's half-cracked, following negative earth energy forces all over the planet, trying to find his dead wife." Melody, or Mel, was not easily diverted from her train of thought.

Chuck didn't think it was at all half-cracked, not even full-cracked, for Doctor Croute to be seeking Mary Croute, his wife. The entire energy force thing, the labyrinth algorithms, everything: it all made perfect sense to Chuck. He tried to explain it to Melody. She nodded a lot, but he had the feeling she didn't quite get it the way he did.

But she did admit, "Well, okay, maybe George's father isn't all that nuts. He is a famous scientist and everything, and, besides, with the weird Einstein's head and cat maze, not to mention that junk in the village with the high walls and smiley face boulders . . . yeah, okay, you have a point. Still, life sucks for all of us, Chuck, maybe in ways you don't realize."

She went ahead of him down the hall back into the living room, where she plopped onto the blue-green sofa. Chuck was puzzled. What was bugging Melody? There wasn't anything wrong in *her* life. He poured a glass of laundromat water and slapped together some peanut butter sandwiches for his friends. The cat was purring on Josh's lap. The evening was almost like a weird party, a prelude of bizarre quiet before a big storm. The night had an odd calm to it, a feeling of no motion. It was eerie. The clock ticked slowly. The laughter of his friends was prolonged. Time was stretching.

He sat on the hard ice covering the snow. With his

arms outstretched, trying to maintain his balance, he stood on the ice, then stooped and slid his feet into the snowboard bindings. He secured the straps. He turned on his portable CD player. Techno music drummed into his ears.

Chuck Farris, video-game superhero, was ready to rock and roll.

With his father's red snowboard strapped to his feet, Chuck had outmaneuvered Digger McGraw and Jack Fastolf, and had saved the town from all sorts of misery.

Chuck passed out the sandwiches, then grabbed the video-game controls from his friends, switched to SSX Snowboarding. He had to smooth his strut, grease his gears, get himself up to speed again. Snowboarding was key; it was as critical as the tardigrades: he felt it in his bones.

He'd already played enough of SSX to understand the general controls. He could grab the board, turn left and right, pick up speed, crouch and jump. He could push other guys off the snow slopes. He did some warm-ups, racing down the slopes alone, flipping, crouching, bouncing off walls until he had a solid grip on the action. Then he turned his attention to the advanced tricks: rail riding, switch, and fakie.

The character-selection screen loaded. Chuck would play again as Mac, who wore baggy white pants, heavy tan gloves, and a blue, yellow, and gray fleece pullover.

The techno music was cranking, giving him the rhythm he needed to block out life and concentrate on the angles of the slopes. People roared "Go go go go" from the bleachers surrounding the starting gates. Chuck's character, Mac, said, "This is what it's all about—showtime!" and then Chuck pressed both joy sticks forward in full throttle, watched the countdown on his screen—5, 4, 3, 2, 1—and they were off!

To make it past the quarterfinals into the semifinals, Mac had to place in the top three out of six snowboarders: Luther, Elise, Kaori, JP, Saskia, and, of course, himself.

Mac flew down the curves, following the red and yellow markings on the snow, gliding to the blaring techno beat. Mac came in fifth, so Chuck played again, and then he came in fourth, and then, finally, he placed third in the race.

Time thinned, stretched, made a great big arc backward, then forward again. Chuck was dizzy. Wispy red angels flew around the room. Big, fiery guys roared from the television screen.

When Chuck woke up, it was midnight. George Croute was on the floor, playing The Bouncer with Josh. George was the character Volt, and Josh was Kou. "We're bar bouncers," Josh was giggling. Oh, brother.

The game was a series of wrestling matches and kung-fu fights all over the city. They were in a rocket cache in some basement. Mugetsu, the bad guy, had Dominique, the girl who kept getting kidnapped from the bar.

Melody was whining. She wanted to unlock Dominique and get to play, too. "Body punches and scorpion kicks, the spinning body blow, the squat kick, and the Dominique bounce. Come on, guys, let *me* play."

"Listen," said Chuck, and everyone turned to look at him, surprised to see him awake again. "We have to get serious. I have some of your dad's software, George."

"The labyrinth algorithms? They were stolen a few days ago," said George.

"I know. But your dad still has the software, and he gave me a copy on a disk."

"Where's the disk?" Josh set his controls on the carpet. "Can you give it to me?"

"Sure." Chuck retrieved it from the closet, where it was still inside the coat pocket. "But what are you going to do with it here, Josh? I don't have a computer."

Josh frowned. "I forgot."

"No problem," said Melody. "I'll go next door and get my mother's laptop. She won't mind. Only problem is, she might keep me there all night."

"Haven't you called her yet, Mel?"

"*Melody*. And no . . . I forgot. She's going to kill me." Melody jumped up, suddenly anxious to rush home. "I mean, she is really going to kill me!"

Josh got a terrified look on his face, too. No doubt, he was considering what *his* mother was going to do to *him* when he got home. "I'd better use your phone, Chuck," he said. "Right away."

Josh called his house, and Melody ran next door. Soon Josh reported that the phone lines were down in the village. And directly after, Melody returned with her mother's laptop. "Nobody's home at my place," she said. "I'm worried, Chuck. Where are my folks?"

"Same place my mother's at, Mel. Probably your

dad's stuck downtown at work in Einstein's forehead or moustache."

She nodded. "*Melody*. And my mother's probably stuck at a grocery store in a maze of giant tuna-fish cans, or something."

"Exactly." He added, "Melody."

"What are we going to do?" she said.

The three boys looked at each other, then at Melody. Nobody had an answer. Everyone was equally worried about their parents, their homes, the town. About life in general. Nothing seemed to make much sense anymore.

Josh gestured at the coffee table. "Put the laptop here, plug it in, keep the PlayStation on."

"What are we going to do?" asked Melody again as she opened the computer, plugged the cable into the wall behind Chuck's TV, and turned on the laptop power.

Josh didn't answer. He pulled the PlayStation memory drive and his floppy disks from his backpack. Then he settled himself on the floor in front of the coffee table. As the laptop came to life, he inserted Doctor Croute's software disk into the machine and scanned the contents. He moved the software onto the laptop's hard drive. He launched the software program.

George helped Josh maneuver through his father's setup. Chuck helped a little, but quickly became silent as he realized that Josh intuitively learned the algorithms in more detail than Chuck had learned them after hours with Doctor Croute.

"I have a PlayStation development tool," Josh explained. "It's a Linux workstation, too." He was beaming as if this was quite a glorious thing, and Chuck was kind of relieved that neither George nor Melody knew what a Linux workstation was, either. Josh continued: "I've been in this closed society for years, it's a software-development group of super-hackers that exists everywhere, but it's so closed that newcomers aren't allowed inside."

"Uh-huh," said Melody and Chuck.

"And I learn how to hack all kinds of cool PlayStation stuff there."

"Uh-huh," said George and Melody. Chuck nodded, not comprehending much of what Josh was talking about or what it meant to the task at hand.

"And they clued me into compilers and linkers, a remote debugger and everything!" Josh was busy, typing commands on Melody's laptop. He had Doctor Croute's labyrinth software running, and he was busy, creating very complex circular and square mazes, so thick with tiny corridors that the mazes were almost solid black with walls. There were mazes that looked like trombones, others that looked like dozens of apples hooked together, still others that looked like fishbowls with sharks in them. Finally, he entered some symbols and numbers, and, voilà, a maze appeared on the screen that made everyone gasp.

It was a maze of Einstein's head. "Watch," and Josh clicked the mouse on a strand of Einstein's hair. A small blinking cursor appeared. The cursor looked like a smiley face. "Sorry," he said to Chuck.

"No problem," Chuck mumbled. How could anyone be as smart as Josh Samson? It was amazing, really, how the guy played with a few numbers, typed some junk, and produced mazes of Einstein's head.

Josh's cursor slinked down the corridor created by the strand of Einstein's hair and took a right near the top of Einstein's head. The cursor traveled down, across, up, right, left, every which way, as Josh wound his way through the maze. "One path," he announced. "It's a labyrinth, not a maze."

"Right," said George, "but just save this thing, would you? Let's get on with it. We can save Chuck's mother and everyone else down in the city later. Don't we have to get to this Labyrinth of Doom place and save the Demon of Runes? Isn't that more important?"

Josh worked feverishly, first saving the Einstein's head maze on his special PlayStation disk drive as well as on the laptop. Then he made a Schnooky's head maze. "The school," he said.

"But how?" asked Melody.

Josh smiled. "Digger McGraw and Jack Fastolf took this software program from George's father, right? So they generated these mazes, or rather labyrinths—both are pretty simple, really—and they probably also generated this Labyrinth of Doom Ice Cap thing where the Demon is trapped. Of course, Digger and Jack are so stupid that they probably created all these Labyrinths of Doom by accident."

"You are one smart guy," said Chuck. The cursor was trailing through Schnooky's head, winding its way into the nostrils and eventually out an earlobe.

Chuck was truly impressed. He was also starting to feel as if there might be a quick end to the latest plague set upon Poultrieville by the two bullies, Digger and Jack. There was hope.

But his hope diminished a bit when George said, "Look, guys, this is all fine and dandy, but we have to get a move on. My dad taught me all about mazes and labyrinths, about negative-energy lines beneath the earth: all of it. Remember, guys, my mother disappeared in a labyrinth and was never found. She may be alive, for all we know, just living in another place and time."

George shook his head sadly, as if wishing for the ultimate joy, the return of his mother, yet knowing it was a near-impossibility to believe that she would ever return alive. "Do you realize—" his voice grew low "—that our very brains are mazes? Think about what your brain looks like: a maze, huh? Now think about your blood system, all the arteries and veins: a giant maze, leading to the heart. And what about your nervous system? Your digestive system? You enter through the mouth and leave through the—"

"Okay, okay, that's gross, George," said Melody. "Keep a lid on it."

George stood and started pacing up and down Chuck's living room. "I have a point, guys. If Digger and Jack can disrupt the city, the school, everything around us, by generating these weird mazes that disrupt the normal energy lines in our world and in the Demon's world, well then—"

"Oh, my god!" gasped Melody, and she finished

his thought: "What's to say they haven't generated mazes that disrupt our bodies, our brains, our guts—everything?"

It was mind-boggling. Chuck gestured at Josh to hurry up with the programming, with whatever he was doing there with Doctor Croute's software programs and the bully's negative-energy mazes and the PlayStation2 console; and his head started whirling again: the Schnooky maze was nothing. What if Digger created a negative-energy maze that destroyed *people*? The bully could cause the deaths of everyone in town, everyone in the city, everyone across the planet.

Surely, Digger would never do that sort of thing on purpose, but the guy was so clueless, so dumb, such a jerk that it wouldn't take much for the moron to trigger the destruction of all life on earth. Including Digger's own stupid life.

Josh hooked up Melody's laptop to the back of the PlayStation console. He stuck something into a back port of the video-game console, muttered something like "Exploder," and attached a cable to the console. "Set BIOS, ROM ready, go go go," and then "Data transfer enabled and engaged," he said like some guy on *Star Trek*.

And that's when the television screen came alive. Mazes spilled onto it, one after another. One particular maze crystallized on the screen and would not budge. It was three-dimensional and circular like a dome on the top. It was all white, at least on the outside. The inside was unknown. It rotated on Chuck's

TV, and water dribbled from the image and formed tiny pools on the . . .

Rug?

How was it possible that water dribbled off a TV image and formed real puddles? The Demon of Runes was at work again, or maybe the world had become so topsy-turvy that everything was messed up.

"What next?" Melody asked the question they were all thinking. She said it in a monotone.

Chuck didn't want to rise to the occasion. He just wanted to crawl into bed, sleep, get up, and play hockey tomorrow. He wanted life to return to normal. But he was the only one, as usual, who could make things right again. Besides, helping everyone else sure beat feeling sorry for himself and moaning about his deadbeat father. Same old story for Chuck Farris. So he said, "Look, you all get some rest while I play TimeSplitters. I'll create the Ice Cap maze of Greenland. I'll find the tardigrades. I'll save the Demon of Runes. I'll stop Digger McGraw and Jack Fastolf from destroying the world. Sound simple enough?"

Nobody said anything for a while. Then Melody said, "We're obviously going with you, Chuck. You're not doing this alone."

"Right," said Josh. "My family has disappeared, too, you know, and George's mother has been gone for as long as he remembers, and his father is—"

"Don't say it," George said, glaring at Josh.

"Sorry, man. Point is, Chuck, we're all in this together, and we're all going with you. So get busy and do your thing, conquer the games, get whatever powers the Demon of Runes guy bestows on you, and get us into the Labyrinth of Doom already."

Chuck had good friends. How stupid of him to think nobody cared when he had friends like Josh Samson, Melody Shaw, and George Croute. Everyone had problems—with a zing of pain and shame, he thought about George's parents—and what mattered was how you dealt with them and with the people around you.

"I'm going in," he said, and alone now on the sofa, he watched Josh nod and trudge down the hall toward Chuck's bedroom, he watched Melody curl into a ball on the floor by the fake-wood banister, and he watched George stretch out on the rug to the side of the television set, with Chuck's cat on top of his stomach.

In silence, Chuck watched the ice dome rotating on his television screen. Chuck wasn't ready to trade in the red shoes for a life of no responsibility for his mother and The Dump; he wasn't ready for a life of giving it all up for nothing. Vengeance is the key? That wasn't the answer for Chuck. If Chuck wanted to get any older, he had to wear his father's old red shoes, he had to beat TimeSplitters and maybe SSX Snowboarding again, he had to find the entry point to the Labyrinth of Doom, get in there, find the center, find the Demon, do whatever he had to do to save everybody. Even old Schnooky, asleep and purring on George's stomach, didn't have a chance of surviving if Chuck didn't pull this off.

SSX Snowboarding came first: he knew that game well and could easily beat it again, gaining his Mac superhero powers. Chuck played the SSX Snowboarding game with only one thing in mind: beat the game, beat the game, and beat the game.

Let me be a superhero again. Give me the power. Come on, I need it, we all need it. Give me the superpowers, give 'em to me.

He went to the Aloha Icejam, plowed through the cliff hazards and across the snow obstacles. He drove his snowboard around the pillars, zipped through the ice tunnels, and soared through the huge doughnuts of ice suspended in the air. He went through the Pipedream: mazes of snow and ice and metal pipes. He zoomed over the ice bowls, avoiding catastrophe, and entered the Merqury City Meltdown, where he ripped between mazes of buildings, avoiding cars, trucks, and buses.

Around light poles and street lamps he flew, and across the glass ceilings. Even the sewer systems were mazes, and the trails through the forest. He went snowboarding through the rock tunnels and subways, and he did all the fancy SSX moves: the flying squirrel, diving moose, plunging porcupine, and twirling turtle. "That's gotta hurt," said some metal-voiced guy over and over again, as Chuck's video-game character nosedived, crashed into poles, and smacked into subway platforms.

He sailed through a giant snowboarding maze that resembled a pinball machine. Stuff shot up from nowhere and started whirling; his character slammed into levers and buttons, walls and sliding boards, Ferris wheels. All sorts of obstacles got in his way, but Chuck was in total control with total focus: he was going to win this game, quickly, as quickly as possible, and graduate to TimeSplitters, and conquer that game, too, tonight. And before dawn, he'd be ready to ride the Labyrinth of Doom to freedom. "Geronimo, combo," said the dead-voiced metallic guy. "You win again!"

Chuck settled back onto the sofa. It was three in the morning. George was snoring on the floor. Schnooky was lapping water from her bowl in the kitchen. Melody's body rose and fell as she breathed, deeply asleep, somewhere inside her dreams. He wondered what she dreamed about.

Ice was pelting the roof and the windows. It'd be tough getting anywhere in the morning. Even Chuck's driveway would be slick with ice. Cars would be unable to move. People would be stranded wherever they were tonight.

Chuck turned his attention back to the screen. He switched to TimeSplitters. He went to the Spaceways, where the music was really cool. He played as R108, the male robot. He ran through total mayhem, and everywhere the walls were yellow, and the carpets were red. It was a nice warm-up for him, and then he moved into challenge mode, and zipped up to the old mansion on Gallows Hill, which was infested with undead spawn: perfect for target practice to get him ready for the ultimate maze—the Labyrinth of Doom in the Ice Cap of Greenland. He beat fifty zombies in two minutes, and he unlocked the next level. He went duck hunting, he grabbed the brain in a box and held on to it for over a minute. He beat every challenge. Finally, he was ready, and he went to the Mapmaker.

No, I can't do this without Josh. I have to wake up Josh. He knows how to generate the very same Ice Cap maze that Digger and Jack made. I have to get Josh.

He paused the game at the Mapmaker and, creating as little noise as possible, left the living room. Ice continued to pound the roof, the windows, the walls of The Dump. Schnooky skittered from nowhere, almost tripping him. She howled. Poor kitty, she was afraid. Chuck scooped her into his arms and murmured comforting kitty things. She was wild-eyed and wrenched from his arms to go skittering back down the hall toward the living room. She slammed into a wall, careened slightly, didn't seem to mind, shook herself, howled, and went flying onto the sofa.

Chuck entered his bedroom. In the dark, the room was eerie. It was weird to see a body in his bed. He shook Josh's shoulders. "Wake up! Come on, buddy, wake up!" he said. Josh refused to get out of Chuck's bed. He squirmed and kept batting Chuck away. Chuck poked his friend, shook him until the bed shook, and then gave up. Josh was not going to get out of Chuck's bed.

As he stepped back into the hall, it seemed to Chuck that his foot took an hour to reach the green carpet. An hour. Time was stretching again—this time, in very long loops. By the time Chuck made it back into the living room, he felt as if weeks had gone by. It was unbearable, this stretching of time. Even Schnooky's howls went on for weeks. His ears hurt. His head hurt. He needed sleep.

On the sofa, he released the video game back into Mapmaker mode, and that's when something odd happened. Time picked up.

And did it ever pick up.

The television screen filled with a hysterically laughing Demon of Runes, whirling like a tornado until he was no more, just a cyclone of dust, and then the Ice Cap maze whirled on the screen like a tornado, until finally it cracked and sprayed George with water, awakening him. George jumped up wildly, screaming from the ice-cold shock, and Melody was awakened by the racket and screamed, and before Chuck could fathom what was happening, Josh was in the living room, screaming, too.

Everyone was screaming. Yet Chuck couldn't move his own lips. He was rooted to the sofa, his fingers gripping the video-game controls, rapidly entering the commands that selected his custom-made maze:

Three levels, all made from ice walls.

On level one, the floor was entirely black: his fingers chose the virtual tile set, glowing black marble. They selected flickering lights in neon colors.

On level two, beneath the cap of the ice dome, he chose Gothic tiles, stained-glass windows, swirling staircase up and down, crosses, eerie walkways, spooky music. He created long corridors with flickering red and blue lights on the stone walls. He created tiny passages that disappeared into black pits leading to nowhere.

There were three-way branching corridors, long hallways, starting positions for his enemies, caches of health. Bright pink neon screaming across orange floors. Spacesport music throbbing in one passage, Gothic music creeping him out in another. Yellow lights, red lights, green lights, blue lights. No lights.

And then on the bottom level, number three, where the Ice Cap dome was widest and oozing water, everything throbbed in black: the floors, the walls, the strange neon green lights with the black cast to them, the cross-shaped holes in stone, the creepy green light shining through the holes, and, deep within the center, a giant green tree holding a giant winged peacock nest. And in that peacock nest: a giant green crystal, cut in hundreds of dimensions, glowing, throbbing, beckoning to Chuck.

He stood. His friends gathered behind him. The house, The Dump, was shaking like crazy. The ice was slamming it from all directions, and time was moving so quickly that Chuck's eyes couldn't focus on the sofa, his friends, the cat: everything was shaking, splitting apart, chinking back together. As one unit, Chuck in the lead, his friends clutching him from behind, they moved toward the front door.

He needed the red shoes. He reached toward the floor, grabbed his father's old snowboard, then twisted the knob on the front door.

Everyone screamed. The cat howled. And in a high-pitched shriek, they all went flying out the front door in a whirlwind of snow and ice.

Your Quest Journal:

1. Save the hockey team from Digger McGraw: **FAILURE.**
2. Find the secret of the tardigrades: **FAILURE.**
3. Go to the Ice Cap: **FAILURE.**
4. Find the Labyrinth of Doom: **FAILURE.**
5. Teach Melody some video-game basics: **SUCCESS.**
6. Learn how to control time: **FAILURE.**
7. Unlock the tenth level: **FAILURE.**
8. Get an escort to Greenland: **FAILURE.**
9. Find the center of the Schnooky maze: **SUCCESS.**
10. Solve the Einstein's head maze: **FAILURE.**
11. Learn how to program complex mathematical mazes on the computer: **SUCCESS.**
12. Solve the sliding-door maze to get out of the village: **SUCCESS.**
13. Find Mary Croute: **FAILURE.**
14. Fence Jack Fastolf with a dowsing rod and win: **SUCCESS.**
15. Force Jack Fastolf to stop selling beer to little kids: **FAILURE.**
16. Wrestle Digger McGraw and beat him with the Batman technique: **SUCCESS.**
17. Find the Genesa Crystal, a.k.a. the peacock jewel: **FAILURE.**
18. Find the secret of the red shoes: **FAILURE.**
19. Beat all the games to get the superhero powers: **SUCCESS.**

Your Inventory:

- Hockey stick
- Photos of hockey heroes
- Memory of the Tower of Darkness world
- Photo of Scott Metcalfe and the Demon of Runes
- Egyptian painting
- Candle in a wall holder
- Ankh
- Screws
- Most Manic award
- Fists of Fury award
- One club
- One wad of dynamite
- *Greenland's Underground Delights*, the textbook
- One broken wok
- Construction worker's hard hat with lamp
- Disk of Doctor Croute's software
- One dowsing rod
- Bright pink jump rope
- Red snowboard

NHL 2001: GAME OVER. NEW GAME?

SSX SNOWBOARDING: GAME OVER. NEW GAME?

SUMMONER: GAME OVER. NEW GAME?

TIMESPLITTERS: GAME SAVED. CONTINUE?

THE BOUNCER: GAME OVER. NEW GAME?

Special Surprise Bonus! Chuck Farris Presents TimeSplitters Tips

Only a few tips this time, guys, because time is moving really fast, and I can hardly think. I'm trying to focus on TimeSplitters right now, so here goes:

You can unlock new characters, such as Fingers McKenzie, Ravelle Velvet, Sebastian Photon, and Angel Perez Bots. If you complete the 1970 Chinese level, you can unlock the Chinese Chef, and if you unlock the 1935 Tomb, then you can unlock the Cultist.

If you complete various challenges, you get all kinds of rewards. For example, if you complete 9-B Flight Delay, then your reward is to unlock the TimeSplitter as a character you can play in arcade mode. To unlock Ginger as a bot in arcade mode, and to reveal the Sorry, Was That Your Bag? level, you need to complete the 7-A challenge, Shop Til You Drop. There are plenty more, but I don't have time right now to tell you about them. I'm whirling in an icestorm toward . . . who knows where?

We're falling. I gotta go!

Chuck Farris

7

ENTER THE FINAL LABYRINTH OF DOOM

Your New Quests:

- ☞ Find the basement of the Tower of Darkness
- ☞ Pick the lock to the castle

Time ground to a halt. Chuck was in midair, and his still-screaming friends were clinging to each other on his back. The ice pellets disappeared. The snow was gone. They were at the tip of the tornado, yet the tornado was no longer whirling. It squirted them from its tip, as if they were nothing more than some birthday-cake icing.

Chuck's body dropped, and he felt weightless, and the drop took no time whatsoever, for time seemed to have ceased. He fell on hard dirt. George fell beside him, Josh landed next, and Melody came down on top of George and Josh. They struggled to their feet.

Where were they?

"Chuck, does this place seem awfully familiar to you?" Josh was brushing dirt from his pants. He'd lost the three top buttons from his shirt. His spare pair of glasses was hanging from his left ear; the right lens was gone. He peered around the forest clearing where they had landed.

"What is this, Chuck?" asked George, turning in a full circle to take in their surroundings.

Heavy maroon clouds shuddered and stretched downward like a trampoline. Then they pulsed upward. They went down and up, down and up, and each time the clouds sank low in the sky, like the underbelly of some giant beast, they shed sweat and dust and stray hairs that fell in long slats of maroon mist to the forest floor.

A pang of horror hit Chuck. He knew this place very well, and though they didn't remember it right now, both Josh and Melody had been here before, too.

"We're nearing the Tower of Darkness," he said. "It's right past this clearing."

"But we're supposed to be in the Labyrinth of Doom!" cried Josh. His face had an odd maroon cast to it.

"I have the feeling we'll be there soon," said Chuck. "Follow me to the castle."

"Castle?" said George. "Where the Demon of Runes lived during the holidays last month?"

"Afraid so," said Chuck, gesturing at the rest of them to follow his lead. They dug through the underbrush and within moments were confronted with the castle known to Chuck as the Tower of Darkness. They paused. "You guys need ammo and equipment. Hold still for a minute. I'll give you some armor, too, and fresh underwear. Don't worry," he added, "I never see what I'm replacing or what's beneath it. Your secrets are safe with me."

Melody blushed. Chuck closed his eyes, concentrated, and then cast the Summoner spells that gave her armor and weapons. He equipped her with heavy armor and leggings, and he gave her several excellent swords. He asked if she remembered how to fence, and she moved back, adopted the en-garde stance, and swooped her sword in great arches and clever jabs.

Then Chuck gave tools to Josh Samson: a spear, the textbook called *Greenland's Underground Delights*, and a clone of his father's red snowboard; and for clothing, Chuck cast the spells that clad his friend in seal and walrus skins and fur. Josh looked like an Inuit.

"How are you doing all this stuff?" asked George.

"When I come here to the Tower of Darkness world, I somehow have all the superpowers of my video-game characters. When I beat the games, I get the powers. The Demon of Runes does this for me. And sometimes I get powers that none of the characters possess. Whatever, I'm able to keep inventory in an invisible mode, just like a video-game character does it, and I'm able to give my friends stuff like swords, shields, health tonics, and food."

George nodded, as if this kind of thing happened every day.

Chuck pulled a root-beer bottle of health tonics from his inventory. The bottle contained the elixir of recovery and the panacea of life. He and his friends drank, passing the root-beer bottle from one to another.

With everyone at full strength and full health, Chuck turned his attention to George Croute, who was the strongest guy there other than Chuck. George could use some excellent equipment: swords, snowboard, hockey stick—you name it, George got it. Chuck really loaded the guy up with health antidotes and medicinal spells, with lock-picking skills, with super-kick abilities, with the power of a world wrestling champion. George's muscles bulged even larger than they were in ordinary life. They were twice their usual size, as were Chuck's muscles. Chuck's arms now fit into George's old coat perfectly, and, if anything, the coat was too small for him. Chuck shed it, anyway. He donned an outfit that had all the toughest attributes from Summoner, The Bouncer, TimeSplitters, and NHL 2001 Hockey. Shoulder pads, knee pads, leather boots, a helmet that looked straight out of Vikingland, and a loose flowing shirt. He pulled out his hockey stick and held it backward, the curved part in his right fist. The other end of the stick was tapered to a sharp point, and the stick itself glistened under the maroon sky as if dripping with blood.

Melody was laughing at him. "You look like a fancy hero from medieval times, who also happens to play football or hockey while brandishing a sword."

"Yeah, well, it'll do the trick," Chuck said. "Let's go." A flush of yellow warmth hit him and flowed down him into his toes. He felt his energy rising to peak levels. He felt his brain focus, become clear, crystallize in some odd way. He was totally sharp, in control of himself. From wherever the Demon of Runes was imprisoned, he was giving Chuck amazing vigor and power.

Beyond the brambles was another small clearing. Here a huge castle rose into the heavens. The bloody maroon sky and clouds were gone. In their place, wispy yellow clouds floated through a lavender sky. As if it had a heartbeat, the castle throbbed, and with each throb the walls bulged, and threads of green fog emanated as if from pores. This was the Tower of Darkness, home of the Demon of Runes. A heavy wooden gate barred their entry. The stone golem sat where it had been before, and over there, by the side of the big gate, Chuck saw the same old spiderweb. As if in a trance, Melody reached out a hand and pulled on the web, and the stone golem melted back into the rustic gate.

Melody unleashed her sword and stepped through the gate onto the moat beyond. Josh and George followed her. Chuck paused by the gate and read the Spanish words, carved in an ancient form of the language. The heading was all in big letters: CONGRATULATIONS. YOU ARE NOW ENTERING THE TENTH LEVEL OF THE TOWER OF DARKNESS.

Did this mean that Chuck was also entering the tenth level of TimeSplitters, the level that didn't exist in the real video game? The Demon had told him it was on the tenth level that Chuck would enter the Labyrinth of Doom.

As he stepped through the gate, following his friends over the moat and onto the grass beyond, he realized that he now had not one but several escorts to Greenland: Melody, Josh, and George. He was at the tenth level, but he hadn't found the tardigrades or the Genesa Crystal. He pulled out his dowsing rod from the invisible inventory sack on his back. He held it in front of him, waiting for the energy lines to pull him forward, backward, sideways: in some direction, any direction.

The Tower of Darkness was not a place for people. It was constructed to keep people *out*. It was a place of refuge for the Demon of Runes. It was his very heart and soul.

Chuck's boots clanked over a metal incline to a giant granite door. Melody tossed a sliver of steel into the mist. She'd just finished picking the lock to the castle. She kicked the door, and it slammed against the inside wall. She darted inside, one fist clenched, the other holding her sword, ready for battle.

Déjà vu: been there, done that. Were they going to replay the entire episode, or this time was something different about to happen? Chuck prepared himself for the worst. They had yet to encounter Digger McGraw and Jack Fastolf, and Chuck felt certain that the two bullies were here, waiting for him.

Chuck stepped into the castle. Where before he had been confronted with a series of stone staircases, all leading up, this time all the staircases spiraled downward into total darkness. As before, the room had no furniture, no walls: just a wide semicircle containing the stone staircases. But as his eyes adjusted to the darkness and the eerie maroon light cast by the sky, Chuck saw something else: in the center of the semicircular floor was a series of stones that looped in a pattern.

He gazed more closely at the stones. They formed a circle, which was divided into four equal quadrants.

The whole thing looked like a math graph from school with the *x* axis carving the circle one way and the *y* axis dividing it in the other direction. In the very center of the circle was a tiny orb of green surrounded by what appeared to be six flower petals. Four of the flower petals were open toward the center, and the other two were partially open. All the stones were flat in the floor.

George pointed at the stone pattern. "It's like the labyrinth at the Chartres Cathedral, where my mother disappeared."

"Which staircase do we choose?" whispered Josh, pointing to the ten paths downward.

Chuck was clueless. He'd been focusing on the labyrinth in the center of the room. "I don't know. There are ten staircases. Maybe they all lead to the same place. Maybe they all lead nowhere. Maybe only one of them is the entry point into the Labyrinth of Doom. Maybe the staircases are meaningless, and the real entry point into the Labyrinth of Doom is this labyrinth on the floor. I mean, that *would* make sense."

George shook his head. His muscles were bigger and greasy-looking. His shirt had ripped at the seams and fallen from his back. He was naked from the waist up. His nose was wider, as were his lips and entire face; his chest was massive and hairy, his shoulders like the shoulders of bisons.

Was George the superhero this time? Or had Chuck simply bestowed him with enormous power?

Melody's armor clanked against the stone wall. She was flat against it, quivering. "Don't come near me,

George Croute," she said. "Something's happened to you, something very weird."

"Huh? What do you mean?" said George. He looked down, saw his chest hair, the muscles, the brawn, and while he seemed startled for a second, he quickly regained his composure and said, "So what? Odd things happen in labyrinths, Melody, and this time we're dealing with negative energies crossing from the netherworld, wherever that is, into our own world, our reality. Look at you, look at Josh, look at Chuck: we're all looking a little strange tonight, wouldn't you say?"

Josh nodded and stroked his seal and walrus clothes. Both his pants and coat were lined with fur. He opened *Greenland's Underground Delights* and sat on the floor in a puddle of maroon light by the castle's front door.

"Books are always good for learning stuff," he said.

Chuck groaned. How would a book tell him which staircase to take? "We don't have time for this, Josh."

"Let him read for a minute. He's a smart guy. He may come up with something." George looked so brawny that Chuck was afraid to disagree with him.

Josh flipped through the pages. Melody sat beside him and scanned the information, too. Both were frowning with concentration. Finally, Josh shut the book. He looked up at Chuck and George.

Josh said, "You'll need that dowsing rod, Chuck. I think the rod will lead us to the correct path down into the earth."

"But of course!" cried George.

"I want you to listen very carefully to what I have to tell you. This is very important," said Josh. "You all know about the magnetic poles, right? North pole, south pole, that sort of stuff."

Melody and George nodded. Chuck remained still, thinking that time was slipping past while they stood here, chattering about geography lessons.

Josh continued: "You know that the earth's magnetic field makes stuff experience an electromagnetic force."

Not really, thought Chuck, *but I'm listening.*

"At the north pole, the magnetic force goes downward, and at the south pole, it goes upward."

Ho-hum. Okay, buddy, what's the point here?

"At other locations on the earth, the magnetic field has a horizontal aspect to it. The field points either toward the ground or away from it at angles."

Chuck was about ready to grab the seal-fur collar and yank Josh up from the floor and scream at him. Instead, he kept his nerves steady, thinking about the missing Mary Croute, the half-mad Doctor Croute, the Einstein's head labyrinth in the city, the Schnooky's head labyrinth that had taken over his school. He remembered the village of Poultrieville, the odd sliding-door maze that consumed it. He remembered how Digger and Jack had gone nuts after stealing the doctor's software and inflicting this mess on the world. Strong tools were in the hands of weak people. Chuck kept quiet, listening, waiting for Josh Samson to reveal the great truths, some key to unraveling the mess.

But George interrupted Josh and continued the little geography lecture. "To make a long story short," he said, "scientists such as my father—who, I point out, is not bonkers—think of the magnetic field around the earth as if it comes from one of those huge bar magnets. The poles of the magnetic field are calculated based on mathematical properties such as direction and strength of the actual magnetic field, and the results, the poles, are known as geomagnetic poles."

Josh was all excited, the way he got in school sometimes when he knew answers to ridiculously hard questions. He almost gurgled with enthusiasm. "Chuck: the northernmost geomagnetic pole is—well, guess where?"

Melody said it at the same time Chuck said it. "Greenland?"

"Yes! Greenland!" cried Josh and George together.

Chuck thought back to what Doctor Croute had told him about ley lines and the dowsing rod. The ley lines were a network of energy beneath the earth's surface, and they originated at great power centers. Pyramids, cathedrals, and other ancient monuments were often located at these power centers. The dowsing rod enabled people to locate the earth energies, the sources of powerful magnetic fields.

And one of those power centers, the geomagnetic pole, happened to be in Greenland. The Genesa Crystal was often a huge source of energy itself, when placed upon a powerful energy center. Any disruption in the natural flow of energy beneath the earth could cause unknown disasters: death, destruction, upheaval as huge as a nuclear bomb.

"Here, let me see that book for a minute." Chuck opened *Greenland's Underground Delights* and scanned the index. Then he turned to page 321 and read aloud: "'There are millions of caves beneath the earth's surface. There are tunnels and caves in volcanoes, glaciers, lava, and in Greenland's Ice Cap. Beneath the Ice Cap itself, the ice tunnels sometimes drop thousands of feet into darkness, and water surges unexpectedly down the tunnels, filling them and the deep pits.'" He looked at his friends. "You obviously all know what this means? There *are* labyrinths beneath the Ice Cap, and they aren't easy mazes like the ones we made in kindergarten. These labyrinths are dangerous: deadly."

Everyone nodded silently: everyone knew what they were facing, and it wasn't exactly a trip to the beach or Christmas at Grandma's house.

Chuck held the dowsing rod outward from his body. Maybe this weird gift from Doctor Croute would lead him to the correct path: either the entry of the floor labyrinth or one of the staircases leading beneath the castle. He shut his eyes. At first, he felt nothing unusual, but then, within minutes, his mind began sinking into a deep concentration, the kind he got—crystal-sharp—whenever he shot a winning hoop in basketball or slammed a puck into the hockey net.

All his energy was focused on his right hand, where he gripped Mary Croute's dowsing rod. Yellow heat flushed up his hand to his arm, into his shoulder, and from there down his entire body. The heat almost knocked him down. It was that strong.

He kept his eyes shut; he refused to open them. He

heard winds whistling, blasts of ocean waves—tidal waves, perhaps—he heard birds singing, he saw the ice-like formations of previous gems and crystals arrayed and glowing with near-demonic force around a circle of loops: the Chartres labyrinth was etching itself into his very being; he felt it, razor-sharp in his mind, coursing through the lobes of his brain, rearranging his circuitry to fit its own—

Chuck was going mad!

He dropped the dowsing rod, opened his eyes. The rod was on the stone floor, glowing maroon, now red, now yellow. It flickered out and dissipated to ash. Chuck's outstretched hand was glowing in its place. He could see his veins, and they were arranged in the palm of his hand and down his wrist in glowing loops of maroon, red, and yellow. And in the center of his palm, just as in the center of the labyrinth on the floor, there was a tiny orb of green.

It did not hurt him. Rather, he felt enormously energized by the experience. His mind was sharp and flooded with images. His body was massive like George's, and he saw that he, too, no longer wore a shirt, that his chest was broad and hairy, that his arms bulged with rock-hard muscles, that his hands were once again like the paws of bears, as they had been when he first entered the Tower of Darkness months ago. His shoes split on all sides and fell from his feet. The soles of his feet were lined with sinew and muscle, and the skin was tough as bear hide. *I could step on nails, and they wouldn't hurt me*, he thought.

Chuck Farris, video-game superhero, had found a

way back into the Demon's lair. This time, it was via TimeSplitters, the construction of the Ice Cap maze in the Mapmaker of the video game, the obliteration of every challenge, every level; the total conquering of SSX Snowboarding, a video game immersed in mazes upon mazes, most of them created from snow and ice.

Most important, the power surged through him because he believed in it. Nothing would stop him from saving the Demon of Runes, from thrusting Digger McGraw and Jack Fastolf back into the real, from shutting the bullies out of the Tower of Darkness forever, so they could never cause trouble again.

He would do it. He would do it with courage, not fear.

"I'm going into the labyrinth," he said, and his voice was deep and loud, causing Melody and Josh to jump slightly, and George to blink rapidly. "When I reach the center, I want you to follow me in this order: George, Josh, Melody. Take your positions in the open lobes: there are four of them. I'll stand in the one that suits me best—you stand in the others. I believe Digger and Jack came here before us; I believe they stood in the two recessed lobes, and they caused a disruption in energy force by building the same Ice Cap maze I created in TimeSplitters, by coming here, by standing in the two lobes allotted for them in the Chartres Cathedral labyrinth, by entering the actual Labyrinth of Doom in this way."

"But how—?" George started to ask.

Chuck cut him off. "I don't know. But when I reach the center of the Chartres labyrinth, I *will* know."

"But what if you disappear inside that thing, like my mother did? What if we all disappear?"

"Go in one at a time, like I said. If somebody disappears, then the next person doesn't enter the labyrinth. Make sense?"

Everyone nodded, but nobody looked particularly convinced of the safety of Chuck's plan. Melody stepped to the entry point of the labyrinth on the floor. "I'm not afraid," she said. "I will go first, if you want."

"I don't know why, but I insist that George go first, followed by Josh, and then you go last, Melody. I don't know why. It is a formation that comes to me through the whorls on the palm of my hand."

From the unreal, I will find the real.

From the darkness, I will find the light.

I begin my journey.

Chuck's massive right foot took one step forward, and his left foot came down next to the opening of the stone path leading into the labyrinth. The stones were set two across, the path was narrow. There were no walls, only stones showing the way.

He placed his right foot upon the first stone inside the labyrinth's path. He placed his left foot on the adjacent stone. Images swam before his eyes. He saw a series of maroon and green whorls leading down a deep tunnel to a bright yellow center. He almost lost his balance and fell into the image: fell into the deep tunnel; and he could feel his body careening down the slopes, bouncing off the sides, bursting into flames as he reached the center, the pit, of that tunnel. He focused; he would not waver from his journey into the Chartres labyrinth.

He saw tangled vines upon trees, tangles that wound around trunks, leading upward, like tangles of a labyrinth or maze. He saw the roots of the trees, also tangled, beneath the dirt, coursing like labyrinth loops to suck energy and water from the ground. He saw music and colors, and then the music danced to the colors, and the colors formed a labyrinth of harmony: the first circuit of the labyrinth was red and was a low C on the scale; and then the second circuit was orange and D; and then the third was the solar flame, yellow, and E; and the fourth: the heart, green, and F; and the fifth: the throat, G, and blue; and then he saw . . .

He was standing at the opening to the whole thing: the opening to a giant living system. It was not merely a labyrinth. It was a gateway, a portal, into something unknown. At the center, the gateway was marked by a Genesa Crystal, the peacock jewel of the Demon of Runes. The main energy forces coursed through the earth from the geomagnetic Greenland pole in a vertical line southward, and directly horizontal, as well, a force slashing its way through the vertical geomagnetic energy line directly where the peacock jewel was placed. The other jewels were here and there, buried within the labyrinth, jewels of yellow, green, blue, and other colors, all corresponding to musical notes and circuits of the labyrinth.

There were portals to ancient times, portals to times ahead. Chuck would have to step around these portals, else he might fall into them, as he often did while playing TimeSplitters. In TimeSplitters, he could enter levels to times and places across history and into the future. Here, it was the same. He would exercise similar cautions, knowing that anything was possible.

The stones undulated beneath his feet. His feet seemed to penetrate the stones and hover on the ground beneath. The ground was cold and solid; it was *permafrost*: frozen forever. Mammoth remains were embedded within the permafrost. *Greenland's Underground Delights*. The pages flipped in his mind. Tunnels and frozen caverns deep within the Ice Cap of Greenland, deep within the maze he had created in TimeSplitters. The two were one and the same.

Chuck was on the right path.

Though the path was flat, he envisioned the walls. He saw statues with beautiful, loving faces: these were the souls who had traversed the Chartres labyrinth before him, and there were many thousands of them. He saw stained-glass windows wavering in the distance, way down the path where it curved and disappeared from sight. And with each step he took, he felt hot springs of energy bursting from the ground beneath the stones. Somewhere, water trickled as if a glacier were melting; and elsewhere, glaciers cracked and thundered down, releasing explosions of ice and frost upon the sea. The energies were misaligned. The Grail Line, originating in southern France and shooting directly through the Chartres Cathedral, was off balance. It was wavering, thinner than it was supposed to be; it coursed in a dizzy fashion rather than with a linear, spear-like thrust.

Was Chuck going crazy like Doctor Croute?

How did he know all this stuff?

Straight he went down the path; then he turned left and followed a curved path until it whipped around and returned him to the edge of stones marking the entry path. He whipped round and round, from quadrant to quadrant, and finally he stepped upon the stones leading to the very center of the labyrinth. The grass was soft and warm. He reached to touch it with his giant hands. It shimmered and released rays of bright yellow energy. It was a peacock jewel.

He remembered the power of the peacock jewel.

It could heal people, it could raise the dead, and it could obliterate bridges—perhaps walls—with one bolt of neon fire.

The jewel was embedded within the grass. It had eight equal segments made from four intertwined circles. It looked like a glowing embryonic creature, the sort of thing shown in science class during lectures about cell division. In this case, the initial cell had divided three times. The first division had created two cells from the first cell; the second division had formed four cells from the two; and the final division had given the jewel eight cells from the four.

It was pretty cool.

Chuck lifted the jewel, and it disappeared into his invisible inventory.

Far behind him, through the eerie, wavering walls of translucent stained glass, through the statues of all who had come before him, Chuck saw George step into the entry point of the labyrinth. His friends were following him. Chuck wondered if George was hoping to find his mother upon the path. Chuck wondered if George *would* find his mother inside the labyrinth. Anything seemed possible right now.

The spell of the peacock floated into his mind. The words made even more sense now than they ever had before:

"coming from nowhere,
going nowhere,
deep within the leaves,
within the frost, the dew, the bark, the pear,
everywhere and nowhere,
all at once.
deep within the soil,
within the clouds,
reaching for nothing,
touching nothing,
and nothing touches it.
alone,
a single gem,
a jewel,
one drop that blazes the way to eternity."

The jewel, in its eight-cell life-form cluster, held within it the potential for infinite life, infinite wisdom, infinite energy, infinite time and velocity, form and space. The jewel held within it a power unsurpassed by anything else in the world.

Chuck remembered what the Demon of Runes told him long ago:

"I gave you the words of the peacock jewel. I can give you only so much."

The Demon had given Chuck *everything*.

As he moved to his position in the first open lobe

of the flower petals within the center of soft grass, Chuck realized that perhaps he had released the energy for his own use, that perhaps he had more to do with it than the Demon of Runes.

Perhaps the Demon had given him the potentials of wisdom, strength, energy, velocity, form, and space; but perhaps Chuck had to use the potentials to make them realities.

Would he know what to do with the peacock jewel and its potentials? Would he use the potential wisely and for good, or would he screw it all up and cause more damage?

George Croute stepped into place inside the open petal lobe opposite Chuck. Soon Josh stood in the lobe next to Chuck, and Melody stood across from Josh. The spaces in the recesses, where Chuck assumed Digger and Jack had stood, were empty. Everything was aligned in space and time. Where would the Demon take them now? And would Chuck know what to do once he got there?

He almost fell. The dowsing rod was jerking violently in his hand. He tightened his grip on the rod. It jerked to the left, and he almost toppled into a wavering statue of a medieval guy. The rod quivered. It swung to the right, steadied, then pointed directly at one of the staircases.

A flush of static hit Chuck. He was supercharged with yet more strength and power. His toes tingled, his fingers, his neck, his scalp. He leapt over the curves of the labyrinth, and in one more leap that spanned twenty feet or more, he whooshed through the air and landed on the top stair.

He heard his friends scrambling behind him. Within seconds, George was there, waiting to follow Chuck down the stairs. Chuck turned and pointed the dowsing rod toward the other side of the semicircle room that contained the labyrinth. The rod quivered again, shifted right and left, then steadied. It was pointing to a staircase directly opposite the one where Chuck stood. Chuck said, "You—Melody and Josh—take that staircase and meet us below."

Josh gulped. "Are you kidding?" He was still inside the labyrinth, and his body was shaking so much that Chuck wondered if Josh could make it out of the labyrinth without falling into the stone markers that framed the path. Chuck didn't dare think about what might happen should his friend fall into the markers. From what Chuck had seen, there were invisible force fields marking the real path, and there were statues and stained-glass windows everywhere.

The stone markers were the only visible pieces, but beneath the surface the labyrinth held energies beyond anything Chuck had ever seen. Even now, the loops of the labyrinth were glowing, as if on fire. Chuck looked at the ceiling, and cast upon the smooth gray granite surface was a glowing mirror image of the labyrinth. Pillars of dusty, glowing light swept upward, extending from floor to ceiling, marking the pattern. Yet something else was there: something was superimposed upon the pattern of the labyrinth glowing upon that ceiling: it was a pattern of—

This time, it was George who gasped. He pointed upward. "It's the same pattern that's on the rose window of the Chartres Cathedral. I've seen pictures of it, photos in my family albums."

Both Melody and Josh still stood within the midst of the glowing three-dimensional labyrinth. Around them, the fires rose, glowed, and above them the ceiling was a spooky etching of what was on the floor clothed in the rose-petal patterns of the Chartres Cathedral window.

Chuck intuitively understood the meaning of the labyrinth, yet he didn't know words to express that understanding. His mind was somewhere else, controlled by someone, perhaps the Demon of Runes. He was still Chuck Farris, of course, and he could feel Chuck inside him; but he was someone or something else now, too, a conglomeration of beings, superheroes from video games, superheroes from ancient history, superheroes that simply rose from the recesses of his own being, forged there by strengths and convictions he wasn't aware he had. He managed to mumble the question "Wh-what is this, George?"

Melody dashed down the path of the labyrinth and streaked from the entry point. Josh followed her. Both sank to the stone floor, breathing heavily, from either fear or exertion, or both. Chuck did not know.

"This is a hopeful sign," said George. "The linear formation and dual energies upon both ceiling and floor indicate that this labyrinth strikes a perfect harmony between masculine and feminine dimensions."

Well, that didn't explain anything to Chuck. Before he could repeat his question, Josh looked directly at George and said, "What *are* you talking about?"

Melody nodded. She rarely said much about masculine and feminine, guy versus girl, and all that other stuff, but she *was* a girl, and if George was about to launch into a lecture about girls as weaklings, or something, Melody wouldn't take very kindly to it.

George said, "Sorry, Melody, and guys, but these are things my father taught me about the Chartres Cathedral labyrinth. He said that this particular formation balances the opposites. He said the curving path represents the feminine in each of us—look, guys, that doesn't mean you're a wimp or anything—and that the sharp turning points where you almost can't move represent the masculine. Well, forget the gibberish if you want, and look at it this way: whether it's masculine, feminine, or whatever, this labyrinth does have coils and very sharp turns. And as you walked it, the forces joined and created this deep positive energy that flooded upward to the ceiling."

Chuck shook his head. Huh? He grabbed George's elbow and pulled him toward the stairway. "Time to go, Mr. Philosopher. We'll take your word for it."

"Whatever your word *was*," added Melody.

"Look, Melody, I didn't mean anything bad by it."

"I know," she said.

"I just—I just think we're seeing a very positive sign here."

"Uh-huh," she said. Melody didn't look particularly convinced.

"If this is in balance, then there's hope. If it were out of balance—for a labyrinth of this kind—then I'd say our quest was fairly hope*less*."

"It makes some sense," Josh conceded. "Don't get all bent out of shape about it, Melody. Everyone knows that girls are more sensitive than guys."

"True," said Melody. "We *are* more sensitive, caring, kind, and compassionate than you guys."

Oh, man, this sounded like a rerun from the days when Chuck's mother and father used to argue about men versus women, for the year or two before his father left them for the bimbo.

His mother: If you live with Chuck and me, if you stay with the family, you can't have girlfriends, Sal.

His father: I can't?

His mother: No, Sal, you can't.

His father, baffled: Why not?

Was this what Melody was talking about?

Chuck was sensitive, caring, kind, and compassionate, at least as much as Melody was; so how come girls always said that boys were insensitive clods? Chuck knew girls who were as cold as . . . well, as the Ice Cap in Greenland. They were like tardigrades, living in permafrost, their arteries and veins filled with some kind of weird antifreeze instead of blood.

Wasn't the entire pathway of your life a labyrinth in itself? You followed the path's curves, the nice steady parts, and then suddenly life got ugly—like your parents got divorced, or maybe something else awful happened, maybe you flunked eighth grade or got kicked out of band, which was nearly impossible to do—and then, after some sharp turns, life got sweet again. Wasn't everyone's life kind of like that? And maybe, in the end, it all balanced out somehow, the good and the bad, the pleasant curves and the hard turns.

In a moment of clarity, Chuck realized that everything was a labyrinth of some kind. Your life, your brain, your blood vessels, your intestines, the stems and roots of trees, the silicon chips and circuitry in computers. If something disrupted the essence of the labyrinth, then everything in life could get disrupted.

Perhaps George was making a lot of sense, after all. Chuck glanced at Josh, the brain, wondering if his friend got it, too; but Josh and Melody both still looked very puzzled.

The dowsing rod bobbed and vibrated, sending shock waves down his body. Chuck had to get moving, or his body might start banging against the clammy stone walls of the staircase. He could break some bones.

"Listen, you two go the way I told you. George will follow me down this side. We'll all meet somewhere in the . . . basement, or whatever's beneath this level of the castle."

Before anything else could delay their journey further, Chuck turned again and bounded down the stairs. He heard George coming behind him. In no time, he reached the bottom.

They were on level one of his Ice Cap TimeSplitters maze. The floor was glowing black marble. Flickering neon lights in many colors dotted the dark granite walls.

"We have to go farther down," he called to George.

Chuck ran through the maze of corridors he had

created using Doctor Croute's software and the Mapmaker portion of TimeSplitters. He knew the maze well. He dodged left and right, ducked at the appropriate times, avoiding robofish bot things that suddenly appeared as if from nowhere; he cringed as he heard George knocking the bot things behind him, cringed as George screamed and grunted and thwacked flying peacocks and catapulting bears. Chuck dodged them all.

They reached a platform, and, in a huge leap, Chuck was on it, and quickly George followed. The platform lowered them into the bowels of the earth.

"Level two," he called.

"Great," said George. "And where are Josh and Melody?"

"Don't know. Hopefully, they're finding their way through the maze. Josh built it using Doctor Croute's software, remember, and so he may know it as well as I do. That's why I teamed him up with Melody, and why you came with me."

They were directly beneath the peak of the ice dome. Chuck had created this level of the TimeSplitters maze with Gothic tiles, stained-glass windows, swirling staircases up and down, crosses, eerie walkways, and spooky music. He had created long corridors with flickering red and blue lights on the stone walls. He had created tiny passages that disappeared into black pits leading to nowhere.

And now he had to find his way through this big mess to get to the bottom level, where he felt he would find an answer to whatever they were pursuing.

There were three-way branching corridors, long hallways, starting positions for his enemies, caches of health. Bright pink neon screaming across orange floors. Spacesport music throbbing in one passage, Gothic music creeping him out in another. Yellow lights, red lights, green lights, blue lights. No lights.

Finally, they reached the platform that would drop them to the bottom level of the Ice Cap.

The platform did not move—not up, not down. It didn't even quiver in place.

"What now?" asked George.

"Don't know," said Chuck.

Where were Josh and *Greenland's Underground Delights* when he needed them?

Perhaps they had to find the tardigrades, the keys to the Labyrinth of Doom. But there wasn't any ice on this level. The main ice corridors were below, in the bottom level of the Ice Cap that Chuck had created.

And then the platform rose—it didn't fall, but rather it *rose*—and Chuck and George went flying while the Spacesport music screeched from somewhere overhead. Chuck landed on hard orange tile. He landed hard enough to smash all his bones, certainly to break his skull, but he felt nothing from the impact, only the pressure against his skin and hair as if he had just settled into his bed for the night. George collided with the floor beside him, and he howled in pain, clutching his left arm with his right hand, unable to squirm or move his legs. George's legs were twisted all out of shape. They were smashed to smithereens.

Chuck pulled his root-beer bottle of health tonic

from his inventory. He forced open George's lips and splashed the tonic into George's mouth. George's face screwed into a "yuck" look, but then he stopped writhing in pain, released his arm, and stood. He was up before Chuck.

By the time Chuck rose from the hard orange tile, the ceiling had crashed down upon them, and falling with the granite were the figures of Melody Shaw and Josh Samson. Both were on the red snowboard. They zipped down the dust and swept across the orange tile, coming to a halt before Chuck and George.

In Melody's hand was the textbook *Greenland's Underground Delights*. She was about to say something to Chuck when another ceiling crash caught their attention. It came from the far right, over where the passageways twined in black and neon pink, and then from the debris another snowboard rose, and on it were the bullies: Digger McGraw and Jack Fastolf.

Your Quest Journal:

1. Save the hockey team from Digger McGraw: FAILURE.
2. Find the secret of the tardigrades: FAILURE.
3. Go to the Ice Cap: SUCCESS.
4. Find the Labyrinth of Doom: SUCCESS.
5. Teach Melody some video-game basics: SUCCESS.
6. Learn how to control time: SUCCESS.
7. Unlock the tenth level: SUCCESS.
8. Get an escort to Greenland: SUCCESS.
9. Find the center of the Schnooky maze: SUCCESS.
10. Solve the Einstein's head maze: FAILURE.

11. Learn how to program complex mathematical mazes on the computer: **SUCCESS.**
12. Solve the sliding-door maze to get out of the village: **SUCCESS.**
13. Find Mary Croute: **FAILURE.**
14. Fence Digger with a dowsing rod and win: **SUCCESS.**
15. Force Jack Fastolf to stop selling beer to little kids: **FAILURE.**
16. Wrestle Digger McGraw and beat him with the Batman technique: **SUCCESS.**
17. Find the Genesa Crystal, a.k.a. the peacock jewel: **SUCCESS.**
18. Find the secret of the red shoes: **FAILURE.**
19. Beat all the games to get the superhero powers: **SUCCESS.**
20. Find the basement of the Tower of Darkness: **SUCCESS.**
21. Pick the lock to the castle: **SUCCESS.**

Your Inventory:

- Hockey stick
- Photos of hockey heroes
- Memory of the Tower of Darkness world
- Photo of Scott Metcalfe and the Demon of Runes
- Egyptian painting
- Candle in a wall holder
- Ankh
- Screws
- Most Manic award
- Fists of Fury award
- One club

- One wad of dynamite
- *Greenland's Underground Delights*, the textbook
- One broken wok
- Construction worker's hard hat with lamp
- Disk of Doctor Croute's software
- One dowsing rod
- Bright pink jump rope
- Red snowboard

NHL 2001: GAME OVER. NEW GAME?

SSX SNOWBOARDING: GAME OVER. NEW GAME?

SUMMONER: GAME SAVED. NEW GAME?

TIMESPLITTERS: GAME SAVED. CONTINUE?

THE BOUNCER: GAME OVER. NEW GAME?

Special Surprise Bonus! Chuck Farris Presents Hot Summoner Tips

A Few Strategies for Joseph

Remember how I turned into part Joseph from Summoner back in the Tower of Darkness? He's the guy I think may be sliding into reality again from the world occupied by the Demon of Runes. He also plays a mean game of fencing.

Joseph is the second-best healer and the second-best fighter in the Summoner group. His job is to summon the creatures, fight at the front lines, and heal/save the party along with Rosalind, another character. Joseph can have large swords and other large weapons once his Heavy Arms reaches level 9.

The area in which to concentrate with Joseph's skills is Sword Weapons. Joseph is better with swords than he is with anything else. It's too bad he doesn't have a Critical Hit category! Even Rosalind does, and she should rarely fight at the front lines! I personally prefer to use two-handed swords with Joseph. In the one-quarter to the one-half part of the game, I prefer to have Joseph use a Katana. In the three-quarter part, I give him a Logaros LongSword, for obvious reasons. However, if you are lucky enough to get the Drithen Sword from Luminar (he sometimes doesn't drop it), then that should be your main weapon with Joseph because there are lots of Frozen Knights and other creatures vulnerable to Fire attacks.

When you get the Sword of Summoners, however, things change dramatically! The Skill Areas you want to focus on mostly are Sword Weapons, Holy, Heavy Arms (get it to a level of 9), and Heal, but Summon is the most important one. You can actually get this skill up to an 18! How? Equip the Summoner's Torque, Summoner's ChainMail, Summoner's Gauntlets, and Summoner's Leggings. Then max out Summon. But, anyway, other than a few points for the usual (Fire, Magic Resist, Parry, Dodge, Double Attack, Dark, and Counter Attack), that should do it.

Finally, because we're talking about fencing—parry, dodge, and so forth—here are some notes about chain attacks: the series of fencing maneuvers that Summoner characters use.

The chain attacks you get with Joseph might fluctuate. For example, in one game, Joseph got Added Blow, Desperation, Push, Confusion, Silence, StaminaAttack, and Revitalize. In another game, he got Added Blow, Desperation, Push, Confusion, Life Leech, Stamina-Attack, Mind Drain, and Silence. In yet another, he only got Added Blow, Desperation, Push, Confusion, StaminaAttack, and Silence. The only way to get more chain attacks is to do a lot of chain attacks. The best chains to use, though, are Life Leech, Mind Drain, Added Blow, and Desperation. These are the ones I generally use. If you want, you can switch to Added Blow with Silence.

We're a little busy right now, but I'll be back later with more tips for you.

Chuck Farris

8

FLOATING FACES, RED SHOES, AND TARDIGRADES

Your New Quests:

- ☞ Meet your fears and conquer them
- ☞ Survive a meeting with Dad and Mom

A huge doughnut made from tan rock rose from the floor, and Josh and Melody's red snowboard turned from Chuck and flew through the hole in the doughnut's center. The snowboard went soaring through the air toward Digger and Jack, whose own snowboard dipped left and under Josh and Melody. Digger and Jack soared through the hole toward Chuck. They stopped so suddenly that they fell from the snowboard onto the orange tiles.

Chuck scrambled into action. He jumped on the snowboard, hoping it would immediately fly into the air and he could magically control where it went. But the snowboard didn't move.

Digger shoved Chuck from the snowboard. He and Jack mounted it again, with Jack clutching Digger's waist from behind. Both were wearing heavy, fur-covered all-body suits. They were dressed for a ride through the permafrost.

"Ha! I made this level, Video Game Boy," said Digger. "Who says you can use my snowboard? Who says you know where your friends are going? The fools."

"Don't you know what you've done?" countered Chuck. "Don't you care that the school is a wreck, the whole city, the fabric of life?"

Digger frowned. He was no longer laughing. "What are you talking about?"

"The school."

"Yeah? What about it? School sucks."

Jack snickered. It was weird how Jack never said anything. He always let Digger McGraw do all the talking for him.

Perhaps the bullies didn't know what they'd done to Poultrieville, to the nearby city, to all the kids and their parents. After all, Chuck hadn't run into Digger and Jack for quite some time now. They hadn't been in the village for quite some time, or in the Schnooky's head wreckage of the school.

"How long have you been here, in this . . . place?" asked Chuck, not knowing how to refer to the Tower of Darkness or the Labyrinth of Doom with Digger and Jack.

This time, both Digger and Jack frowned. Jack grunted slightly. His breath came from his mouth in a stream of fog.

The temperature was dropping rapidly.

Because he'd been racing at top speed through the Labyrinth of Doom, and because he was wearing arctic clothing, Chuck hadn't noticed the drop in temperature.

How low would it go? More important, how safe were they down here? Would the temperature drop so low—say to negative five hundred degrees—that they'd all turn into ice statues?

Digger fingered the fur-covered jumpsuit button on his waist. His whiskers had grown very long. He had a full beard. His forehead was as wrinkled as that of an old man. How had the creep aged so much in such a short amount of time?

Was it due to TimeSplitters? Was it due to the wedge between reality and the Tower of Darkness world? A combination of the two?

"I don't know how long we've been down here, Chuckie boy," said Digger. "What happened in the school?"

"It's more like what happened *to* the school," said George, who had recovered from his "accident." George hollered to Josh and Melody to return from wherever they'd gone inside the labyrinth. But Josh and Melody didn't return, and they didn't call back to him, either. "I'm going off to look for them," said George. "They might be lost in the labyrinth. Maybe it's a freaking maze now. Or they might be hurt, crashed on that red snowboard—" He raced into the opening that led into the labyrinth. It happened so quickly that it almost seemed that the labyrinth opened, yawned a great dark hole, and swallowed him.

Too much was happening and too quickly for Chuck to take it all in, analyze it, sift through it, and determine a logical course of action. He explained briefly what was going on back in reality.

"We didn't do any of that stuff," said Digger.

"But you stole Doctor Croute's software, didn't you?" said Chuck.

"Yeah."

"And you ran it and found a giant Ice Cap labyrinth thing, didn't you?"

"Well, yeah. What of it?" Digger seemed genuinely puzzled by Chuck's questions. Jack had ceased grunting. The two got off the snowboard and set it against the back wall by the opening to the labyrinth.

"Did you happen to master TimeSplitters?" Chuck already knew the answer, but he had to hear it from Digger McGraw.

"Sure I did," said Digger.

"And you went into the Mapmaker?"

"Sure."

"And you re-created Doctor Croute's Ice Cap labyrinth thing?"

Digger nodded his head. *Yes.*

And then Digger slapped his forehead with his right hand. Chuck half-expected Digger to say "Duh," but the bully turned and stared at his friend, Jack Fastolf. Jack was clueless. Digger said, "Jack, don't you see?" Jack didn't see; he never did. So Digger said to Chuck, "I see what you're saying now. Okay, I admit that I came back here, *on purpose*, to find the Demon of Runes again. I like it here. I hate it back in school, in town."

"So you found the Demon?"

"Yeah, it wasn't hard. I mean, I didn't know what happened back in Poultrieville. I wouldn't do something like that on purpose. I wanted to come *here*. I didn't want to be *there*. But I didn't want all this negative-energy crap you're talking about to sift into the real world and destroy it, or kill people, or whatever. I'm no killer, Chuck. Are we, Jack, *huh?*"

"Who cares?" It was Jack. He actually said something. Chuck couldn't believe what he was hearing—Jack Fastolf opened his mouth and uttered words. Jack followed his two words with a loud grunt and sneer.

Digger suddenly looked sly. He sneered, too. "Yeah, with the town busted and the school shut down, kids will be bored to death. They'll buy more stuff from me."

"Or from me," said Jack.

"They'll want drugs," said Digger. "Crack and dope, cigarettes." He was laughing.

"They'll want beer," said Jack. "Forget the cigarettes."

"You big jerk," said Digger. "Who wants beer if you can get drugs?"

Chuck had heard enough. The two creeps were *really* getting on his nerves now. There they were, standing there all high and mighty, arguing about drug, cigarette, and beer sales to kids. Chuck felt like punching them both into pulp. "You idiots! If the town is destroyed, if nobody can get out of it, everyone will die! Nobody will be alive to buy your stinking drugs and stupid beer! What idiots! I swear, you two are the most stupid, *stinking* idiots I have ever met!"

"Calm down," said Digger. "Any kid with half a brain would rather be here than in school or back at home. Maybe we should find a way to get all the kids here in this place and out of the real world."

Chuck blinked. The bully had a point. If given the choice of being here or—

Now, wait a minute. No kid would prefer a dark, cold, scary place to sun, snow, a warm bed, and food. "There's nothing to eat here," Chuck pointed out.

"Sure there is. Remember the berries and stuff out in the woods?"

Yeah, Chuck remembered: he'd eaten plenty of magical stuff, too, when he first came to the Tower of Darkness world. He was sick of arguing with Digger. All Digger thought about was personal gain and making other people feel bad. Chuck had to get to the final level of the Ice Cap labyrinth.

He gazed around at the second level. The tiles were neon orange and black, and they formed a pattern of some kind. Stained-glass windows cast eerie lights here and there in the murkiness, illuminating staircases that wound up or down. The music was beginning to spook him. It droned on and on in the background, like a mantra. There was a black pit somewhere, he'd put it here when he made the maze using the Time-Splitters Mapmaker. If he could just remember where the pit was, where the level flowed into the final one . . .

Digger and Jack hovered over him on their snowboard. They were aimed away from the level, toward the platform. "Don't forget, I made this level, too," said Digger, and then the two bullies shot through the air to the platform, and the platform began to lower.

Chuck ran as fast as he could, and with his superpowers that was pretty fast, but still, as he made a giant leap toward the lowering platform, he missed; somehow, he missed. Sure, he landed on Jack's back, he should have descended to the lowest level with them, but his body fell through Jack's and then through Digger's and then straight through the snowboard and through the platform itself. He landed in a pile of snow.

The bullies did not follow him. He craned his neck to look at the ice ceiling. Whatever had dropped in here had left. The platform was no more.

Turquoise and bright blue lit the frost around him. He was in a giant cave of snow and ice. Below him was a drop straight into the pit of the earth.

He was inside the Ice Cap.

A face far beneath indicated that someone had been here before him. The face was frozen in fear. Was it attached to a dead body?

Something echoed off the ice walls of the pit. Chuck was in a hollow place, alone, with no way out. He was hearing things. What could possibly be talking or howling or whatever in a frozen place like this? Yet he heard it. There it was again—a long, low howling, like a wolf dying through a long night. Again, it seemed that time had slowed, as if the howling was stretched like taffy through time, as if time itself had been stretched; and Chuck had a moment of terror: what if time suddenly snapped back in place?

The howling continued. The frozen face continued to stare at him from hundreds of feet below in the pit of solid ice.

Sweat dripped down Chuck's back and beneath his pants. It quickly froze, sending him into the shakes. He rubbed his arms, trying to calm himself and warm his body.

He was afraid of heights.

He sat on the ice, carefully keeping his legs from dangling over the precipice. The ice was brownish, tinged with something. The brown scraped across the bottom of his pants legs and across his rear end. Across the pit from him was a horizontal tunnel filled nearly to the top with water.

From his inventory, Chuck pulled the construction worker's hard hat and screwed the carbide lamp tightly into the front of it. His fingers were now clad in thick, fur-lined gloves; yet they were still nearly immobile from the cold. He managed to switch on the lamp. A warm yellow glow filled the frozen white space. Now he needed some rope. He pulled Candy Malone's jump rope from his inventory, and, to his delight, it was no longer short and pink; rather, it was as tough as sinew, very long, and very lightweight. He had metal screws somehow collected by his cat, Schnooky, from all over The Dump and left in a heap for him by the front door. He hammered a few screws into the ice behind him on the wall, then a few more into the ice lip of the deep ravine.

The jump rope had clips on the ends, and Chuck attached the clips to the metal screws. He had some sort of spring-loaded device in his inventory. He called that item forth and strapped it to his back. It was like a backpack, the kind he wore to school, except it had gears all over it. He did not want to drop down this pit. He did not want to swim through near-freezing ice-slush water, either. And there were no other options.

Here goes, he thought. *I'm dead meat, for sure. I didn't put this on the final level in TimeSplitters. This is not my level. This must be Digger's version of the same thing, and I don't know what he put into this maze or labyrinth, how to make my way through it, or what I might find.*

The ice began rumbling. Then it began shaking.

Chuck remembered what he'd read in *Greenland's Underground Delights*. There were millions of caves beneath the earth's surface. There were tunnels and caves everywhere: in volcanoes, glaciers, lava, and in the Ice Cap itself. There were pits dropping thousands of feet in darkness. There was water everywhere, too; it could fill these pits one week, then empty into long tunnels the next.

What if the place where Chuck now sat suddenly filled with water? After all, the tunnel across the pit from him was filled with water. Who was to say that water wouldn't suddenly flood Chuck's chamber?

Chuck was submerged inside three hundred trillion tons of ice. He had to get out of here. Not only was he afraid of heights, he realized that he was also claustrophobic, not to mention starving and tired. Forget saving the stupid Demon of Runes, the village, the city, and all the rest of it. Chuck would be lucky to emerge from this place alive.

He trained his carbide lamp beam into the pit. The face was still there, unmoving. Would Chuck suffer the same fate? Would he drop into the pit, never to return?

Condensation from his breath froze on his coat sleeves and his collar. He looked up, hurting his near-frozen neck from the effort. Where the platform had been, now there were icicles, dangling and trembling, ready to break off and descend, to skewer his body to the frozen ledge.

He tried to stand. He was still rocked by fear and too frozen by the sub-zero temperature to move his legs. Beneath him, Candy Malone's transformed jump rope was encrusted in ice.

I'm going to die, he thought. *These are my last few moments on earth . . . or wherever I am.*

What an awful way to go. He was laughing hysterically on the inside, but unable to open his lips and let the sound out.

Hey, Dad, you got the last laugh, didn't you? I won't get any older, but you will. You're still wearing the red shoes, Dad. Those were my shoes you took. I'm supposed to wear the red shoes—me, not you. I'm the kid—me, not you. Why'd you have to stick me with all this?

His hysteria gurgled and spilled over into the need to weep. But he couldn't do that, either. His eyelashes were frozen open, his eyes couldn't form tears.

The angels have swiped my red shoes, Dad. And they gave them to you.

Something flickered in the tunnel of water. It was the face of his mother, followed by her body. Chuck was getting delirious, losing his sanity, alone here, freezing literally to death in this horrible Labyrinth of Doom.

His mother was wearing a long, gray, wispy nightgown. Her hair hung in glossy black spirals to her waist. This was the way Chuck's mother had looked before he was born. He was losing his mind.

She wasn't wet from the water. She didn't look cold: her face was flushed pink, her eyelids were blinking, her lips were moving . . .

"Chuck, my Chuckie, how I've always loved you. I wanted you to have a good life, Chuck, and I failed. I failed miserably."

She flew across the divide, from the tunnel of near-frozen water to the cliff where Chuck was frozen to the ice. Her skin was soft and warm. She brushed her fingers across his cheek. He couldn't feel her touch him. He was rooted in place, unable to move at all, growing increasingly impervious to the cold; he was having visions.

His mother sat beside him and put her arms around his body, and she hugged him. She wore no shoes. Her toenails were painted with bright pink polish.

Another figure was floating across the divide from the tunnel of water. Chuck wanted to die.

It was his father.

He, too, was much younger than he probably looked now. Chuck hadn't seen his father for seven years, and he was too young back then to remember things well. Of course, Chuck had seen plenty of photos of his father, and this figure floating toward him was the twenty-year-old version of Dad.

The figure wore red shoes.

The figure—was it really his father?—was dressed in modern clothes, new stuff, the latest styles: low-slung baggy shorts, cool sneakers, and a blue-green knit shirt that was the color of his eyes. Red whiskers sprouted from his cheeks and chin, and he had a wide, bushy red moustache. He looked like a slightly older Chuck.

His father sat on the other side of Chuck, and embraced him, too. Beneath Chuck's chin, across his torso, his parents were clasping each other's hands. His father's right thumb had a scar near the nail. A whiff of Ancient Spice penetrated Chuck's frozen nostrils.

Help, he wanted to cry, *help me, one of you, please help me.*

"You don't have to go down into that pit," said his mother. Her lipstick matched the pink on her toenails. Her breath was warm on his cheek. It didn't condense into icy fog streams.

"Stay up here with us, Chuck," said his father. There wasn't even one flake of snow on his moustache. Not a single particle of ice in his hair. His bare legs were stretched across the solid ice ledge. They were tanned and possibly tinged with sunburn.

What are you doing here?

"I've come to help you."

But why now? Where have you been all these years? How could you do that to Mom and me, Dad? How?

"I can always come to you, Chuck, even after I die."

What are you—a ghost or something?

"No."

Mom, are you dead? Mom, did you get out of the dentist's office downtown? How did you get down here? Why do you look so young? It's hard to look at you, Mom. I never knew you were so pretty when you were twenty.

It was painful to look at his mother, only seven years older or so than Chuck was now. She looked like some babe from the music channel at Josh Samson's house.

"The angels took my red shoes when I married your father. They never gave them back to me. I don't think I've ever been happy, not since you left, Roger."

Chuck's father floated around Chuck and grasped his mother. She released Chuck and hugged . . . Roger.

Roger? This was *too* freaky. Chuck's father was named Sal, short for Salvidore, an exotic kind of name, Chuck always thought.

This guy here, this figure, wasn't Chuck's father.

"Yes, I am," said Roger. "Face it, boy. Your father's long gone. He didn't *want* to be your father."

No!

"He didn't love you or your mother here."

No!

"He left you. He left you, Chuck Farris."

"No!" screamed Chuck. His voice shattered the icy silence of the giant pit beneath them. He leapt to his feet, turned this way and that, but the two figures were gone. On the ice, where he'd been sitting, was a mat of soft brown. It was undulating, snagged by the ice but waving slightly from the draft left by the two ghost-like figures. Chuck stooped and touched the mat. It was scorching hot.

He wished for the mat to enter his inventory, and it disappeared from the ice ledge, just like that.

He was warm, he was fine. It was as if something had filled him with some weird antifreeze. He checked his inventory. He could mentally do that, as if he were Joseph from Summoner. The soft brown mat was algae, and it was coated with microscopic tardigrades. The tiny animals lived on algae, sucking the stuff into snouts that looked like boring drills. The tardigrades were puffy, like marshmallows that have been melting on a stick over a fire. They were adorable. *Tardi*, slow; *grado*, walker: Chuck remembered what Melody had taught him that night on the phone.

Thoughts streamed through his mind, one after another, in a steady pulse:

I want my red snowboard. But Josh and Melody still have it, and they're still lost on the upper level of the labyrinth. Well, maybe I'm not going to die just yet, after all. Maybe these tardigrades have helped my body tolerate this permafrost and this tundra place. I'm going down to see that face in the pit. Why should I be afraid? For all I know, maybe I'm already dead. What was that Roger guy talking about?

Chuck slid down the rope toward the face down there in the blackness of the pit. His feet scraped the ice wall, dislodging a chunk of ice the size of his refrigerator. The ice block crashed downward, banging against the sides of the ice cliff, smashing into the darkness, colliding with something way down there: maybe the bottom of this thing. The face was still down there, he saw: still illuminated by the carbide lamp strapped to his hard hat.

It was at the bottom that he found there really was no bottom. He made it to the face, but it wasn't really a face. It was another image, a figure of ghost-like appearance: a trick of light played upon the ice to make Chuck think he was seeing a face. It was supposedly a face not unlike his mother's. This face was disembodied; that is, when he dug around the ice where the face was lodged in the side of the ice wall, he found that the face wasn't attached to a body. It didn't even have a neck. It was like a sheath of skin with a nose sticking out of it, and lips, and nostrils . . . that breathed.

Chuck almost let go of the rope. He stared closely at the face thing. Its lips moved. "I am Mary Croute," it said.

Yeah, right. Enough is enough, Chuck thought. *You're Mary Croute, George's long-lost mother, the same way that I just saw my parents still in love when they were twenty years old.*

"Find the rest of me. Find the Demon of Runes."

Chuck sure hoped his friend George Croute hadn't run across this thing. It was freaky enough to see Chuck's mother floating around down here in one solid mass, but imagine if he'd seen only her face.

Chuck lowered his head so the lamp would shine farther into the pit. On the bottom level, number three, where the Ice Cap dome was widest and oozing water, everything throbbed in black: the floors, the walls, the strange neon green lights with the black cast to them, the cross-shaped holes cut in the ice, the creepy green light shining through the holes, and, deep within the center, a giant green tree holding a giant winged peacock nest. And in that peacock nest: a giant green crystal, cut in hundreds of dimensions, glowing, throbbing, and beckoning to Chuck.

Your Quest Journal:

1. Save the hockey team from Digger McGraw: FAILURE.
2. Find the secret of the tardigrades: SUCCESS.
3. Go to the Ice Cap: SUCCESS.
4. Find the Labyrinth of Doom: SUCCESS.
5. Teach Melody some video-game basics: SUCCESS.
6. Learn how to control time: SUCCESS.
7. Unlock the tenth level: SUCCESS.
8. Get an escort to Greenland: SUCCESS.
9. Find the center of the Schnooky maze: SUCCESS.
10. Solve the Einstein's head maze: FAILURE.
11. Learn how to program complex mathematical mazes on the computer: SUCCESS.
12. Solve the sliding-door maze to get out of the village: SUCCESS.
13. Find Mary Croute: SUCCESS.
14. Fence Digger with a dowsing rod and win: SUCCESS.
15. Force Jack Fastolf to stop selling beer to little kids: FAILURE.
16. Wrestle Digger McGraw and beat him with the Batman technique: SUCCESS.

17. Find the Genesa Crystal, a.k.a. the peacock jewel: **SUCCESS.**
18. Find the secret of the red shoes: **SUCCESS.**
19. Beat all the games to get the superhero powers: **SUCCESS.**
20. Find the basement of the Tower of Darkness: **SUCCESS.**
21. Pick the lock to the castle: **SUCCESS.**
22. Meet your fears and conquer them: **FAILURE.**
23. Survive a meeting with Mom and Dad: **SUCCESS.**

Your Inventory:

- Hockey stick
- Photos of hockey heroes
- Memory of the Tower of Darkness world
- Photo of Scott Metcalfe and the Demon of Runes
- Egyptian painting
- Candle in a wall holder
- Ankh
- Screws
- Most Manic award
- Fists of Fury award
- One club
- One wad of dynamite
- *Greenland's Underground Delights*, the textbook
- One broken wok
- Construction worker's hard hat with lamp
- Disk of Doctor Croute's software
- One dowsing rod
- Bright pink jump rope
- Red snowboard

NHL 2001: GAME OVER. NEW GAME?

SSX SNOWBOARDING: GAME OVER. NEW GAME?

SUMMONER: GAME OVER. NEW GAME?

TIMESPLITTERS: GAME SAVED. CONTINUE?

THE BOUNCERS: GAME OVER. NEW GAME?

Special Bonus! Chuck Farris Presents Hot Summoner Tips!

Many people have emailed me to ask, "Any tips on defeating Mortankas the Lich?" Well, here's your answer. You don't need to prepare for this at all. You find old Mortankas in an Icelands Random Encounter after you have the Seventh Tome Page. There are two known ways to accomplish this. The answer is incredibly simple, but not obvious.

The first time I played the game, I summoned the Dragon of Forest. The Dragon of Forest empowers your party and does 30 damage to Mortankas. You can do this six or eight times, and Mortankas will fall. Unfortunately, it takes 30 AP each time you summon the Dragon of Forest (or any dragon), and Joseph most likely won't have 180–240 AP by then.

The easiest way is simply to summon the Jade Golem and use his attack, Jade Beam. This does less damage, but it only takes 15 AP (I think) to summon the Jade Golem. If you're looking for the Eighth Tome Page, Mortankas is most likely to drop it off the ledge that he's on. So you can just run down and pick it up.

Because I receive so much email about Summoner, I'll probably end up putting a more thorough Summoner strategy guide on the Web. I think something like 2,500 guys come to my Summoner strategy guide

Web page every month. That's a lot of guys. Summoner is still one of the best PlayStation2 games. I never get tired of it.

TimeSplitters is awesome, too.

I wonder why Digger McGraw likes the same video games I like. That kind of freaks me out.

There's one final thing I want to tell you guys. All this stuff about labyrinths and mazes happens to be true. A lot of people, including scientists, study energy sources beneath the earth and even the Ice Cap, and they find balances in the energy that they believe keep the planet stable. All those mazes and pits beneath the Ice Cap are really there. The tardigrades are real, too.

Until next time—

your friend,

Chuck Farris

9

ALL ROADS LEAD TO POULTRIEVILLE

Your New Quest:

☞ Survive once again

It was the peacock jewel owned by the Demon of Runes. It was also the Genesa Crystal, smack dab in the center of the Labyrinth of Doom. Sitting in the peacock's nest was Mary Croute, her face now attached to an entire body. She was wearing sandals and shorts, and a loose shirt with a collar. Her hair was brown and straight, and was held behind her neck with a rubber band.

Also in the nest was a fiery guy with big muscles. He wore a breechcloth. He had red eyes and worm-like hair. He was the Demon of Runes.

"At last," said the Demon of Runes. "I thought you'd never get here. I want to go back to my castle now. Unleash me. Please."

"Where are my friends?" asked Chuck.

"They are safe back in Poultrieville. As you dropped to the tenth level beneath the ice crust—"

"*Tenth* level?"

"Yes, the level you and Digger both created in TimeSplitters. You entered his version down here at the bottom, where he trapped me weeks ago. Well, as you dropped to this place, this pit where Digger trapped me, you also obtained the power of the tardigrades to withstand the arctic force."

I don't understand.

"Once you broke past the tenth level, once you got here with the power of the tardigrades, you set me free from the mess Digger and Jack created. You see, Digger threw me into this pit, but he couldn't get down here to check on me or to get me out. He didn't want to trap me here forever. He's an idiot."

No kidding. But—

"He was wrestling me, he and that stupid oaf, Jack Fastolf. They wanted to beat the Demon of Runes at The Bouncer. Fat chance. I knocked Jack to his face, and I almost did the same to Digger. But then they tried fencing me with Summoner swords. I'm all off balance. The split between my world and your world has damaged me, too. Just as the energy of my world has permeated your world, the energy of your world has permeated mine. I lost the struggle. I fell off the ledge up there into this pit, where the center of all energy resides in the earth: this Genesa Crystal, the peacock jewel of All Power. Infinite power, the jewel has, yet it's everywhere and nowhere all at once, if indeed you are its owner."

Chuck remembered the power of the peacock jewel. Without full control over the jewel's power, with the juncture wide open and time and energy oozing between this world and Chuck's world, well, it was easy to understand how the Demon of Runes had lost his balance and fallen into this pit.

"Once you started descending here, I regained sufficient power to force Digger McGraw and Jack Fastolf out of my domain and back to Poultrieville Middle and Senior High School. The other two, Josh Samson and Melody Shaw, are also back in school. Only you remain down here."

"What about my parents, and Mary Croute here?"

The Demon hopped from the peacock nest and helped Mrs. Croute down, too. She smiled at Chuck. "I'm not real," she said. "When energy gets all screwed up like this, anything can happen."

The Demon explained further: "I'm real, Chuck, that you know. However, remember that you're in a Labyrinth of Doom that Digger McGraw built for you to follow in TimeSplitters. You know how you put robofish, bots, monsters, health, obstacles, and whatever into your labyrinth?"

Chuck nodded.

"Well, Digger put stuff into his labyrinth, too. He put computer-generated images of Mary Croute—which he obtained from poor Doctor Croute's computer programs—and of your parents, which he created easily with the doctor's programs—"

"But how did he know what my parents looked like? And why did he call my father Roger?"

The Demon of Runes laughed. He held Mary Croute's hand. "I won't know you for much longer, my dear," he said to her. "But it's been nice having some company for a while. *I've been very lonely for a long time.*" And to Chuck: "Doctor Croute's software generates these figures. It can store a photo of someone, then generate an image from it. That's how the doctor originally created the figure of his dead wife, Mary Croute. Sorry, my dear, but you are lovely, even dead. Digger knew what your mother looks like now, Chuck, and he knows what *you* look like. He simply asked Doctor Croute's software to generate younger versions of these two images. He didn't know your father's real name, that's all."

A boom, like thunder gone mad, split the underground tomb where the deceased Mary Croute, the Demon of Runes, and Chuck stood. Ice slivers rained from above, slashing the Demon's face, arms, and torso with bloody gashes. Mary Croute was untouched, or, if the ice hit her, it didn't cut her, it simply melted or slipped through the ephemeral essence that was her body. After all, Mary Croute was unreal, a figment of Digger McGraw's TimeSplitters maze.

As for Chuck, the ice hurt plenty. "Get me out of here!" he cried to the Demon of Runes. "Get me out now, before this stuff kills me!" As he yelled for help, another chunk of ice crashed down from above, smashing at his feet. Chuck leapt back, slammed into the ice wall that stretched hundreds of feet upward. There was no scaling that wall, and Chuck had never played a video game that gave its hero the ability to fly.

The Demon stretched his arms upward. "Go back, Chuck Farris, and close down the portal to my world. Stop Digger McGraw from coming here again."

But as long as Digger plays video games as well as I do, the door will remain open. He'll find new ways to get here, simply by mastering tough new games and pushing them to their limits. He'll find a way. How will I ever stop him?

This time, nobody answered Chuck's thoughts, nobody helped him grope for the truth. The Demon blasted him back to reality.

The Demon blasted him straight into the state semifinal hockey game between Poultrieville and the high-class wonder team from Buffalo.

Chuck was in the center of the rink, skating like crazy toward the Buffalo goal. Some huge guy—was it Digger again?—came out of nowhere and slammed Chuck's body with his hockey stick. Chuck winced and nearly fell from the impact, but he kept his ground and kept control of the puck.

The hockey mask on the attacker's face gave the guy the look of a giant man-eating insect. Huge pimples on his nose glistened beneath the glow of the overhead rink lights. His eyes squinted, and drops of sweat beaded on the protruding ridges of the mask. He lifted the hockey stick over his head.

Was it Digger?

No, the guy wasn't wearing the blue jersey of the Poultrieville team. It wasn't Digger, it was some Digger-like creep from the other team. Chuck swerved and ignored him, raced right past the guy as if racing past a ghost. He zoomed toward the goal, and his friends in the stands rose and cheered. "Go, Chuck! Come on, go!" Melody Shaw and Josh Samson were jumping up and down, screaming his name.

A few blue jerseys zipped into view: Al and Tony and Vince. Chuck slapped the puck into the goal—

wham!—and to his astonishment the end-game whistle blew, and he looked at the score: Poultrieville had lost the game.

What? How?

The score was Buffalo 23, Poultrieville 1.

Chuck had scored the only goal.

Where was Coach Flanders? Chuck turned and saw the coach sitting by the Poultrieville goal with Mr. Viking, the janitor, and the principal, Mr. Calhoun. George Croute was manning the goal. He looked as baffled as Chuck felt. Along with the grown-ups were a bunch of kids who never played on the Poultrieville team. Apparently, these guys had been playing for Chuck and George Croute while the two were in the Labyrinth of Doom. No wonder Poultrieville had lost. By the time Chuck and George returned to play in the game, all was lost.

Digger and Jack were not on the team. Chuck wondered where they were: selling beer and drugs, cigarettes, and other bad times to the little kids down the road at the elementary school?

Chuck skated into the locker room, removed his skates and jersey, opened his locker. His body and face were back to normal. They no longer rippled with the muscles of a steroid-pumped super-athlete, or rather with the power of a video-game superhero. As he had last time, he felt a surge of relief that he was once again just plain old Chuck Farris, ordinary kid.

George Croute skated into the locker area from the rink and pulled off his skates. He sat on the bench beside Chuck and shook his head. "That was one weird game," he said. "I mean, it was over before it began. I don't remember anything happening, Chuck, except for those last few minutes, when we lost to Buffalo. I must be going daffy or something."

George looked like himself again, too. Sure, he still looked like a worldwide wrestling champion, but then George always looked like a worldwide wrestling champion.

Chuck pulled a towel and washcloth from his locker, and headed for the showers. He called over his shoulder, "Yeah, I know, George. It was the worst game we ever had."

Then George said something that made Chuck look back and stare at him. "You know," said George, "I'd swear my mother was in the stands, watching the game."

"Did you see your mother?" asked Chuck.

"No . . ."

"Then what makes you think she was here?"

"I don't know, Chuck. It almost feels as if I spent the game with my mother instead of playing it. I can't explain."

"What did she look like?"

"I can't even tell you that much. I don't know."

Chuck sighed and went into the showers, turned on the warm water, grabbed the soap from the tray in the wall. Apparently, George and the others would remember nothing about the Labyrinth of Doom, just as nobody except Digger and Chuck had remembered anything about the Tower of Darkness last month.

Emerging from the locker room half an hour later,

Chuck and George walked silently together through the halls of Poultrieville Middle and Senior High School. It was quiet now, as most of the kids and their parents had gone home. George was still in a daze, so Chuck kept quiet. He had his own thoughts: the school was no longer a maze of Schnooky's head, the principal's office wasn't lined in fur, there were no wet nostrils near the front door. Was life normal again? Had the seam between reality and the Demon's world been secured?

Doctor Croute was waiting outside in a fancy sports utility vehicle. He called to George, then to Chuck. He looked haggard, more tired than Chuck had seen him earlier . . . was it today, yesterday, or two weeks ago when Chuck had entered the Labyrinth of Doom? All notions of space and time were totally warped. Though time seemed to be moving normally again, no longer stretching and thinning into the void of tomorrow.

The doctor asked if Chuck wanted a ride home. Chuck nodded. "Sure," he said. "It will save me a hike down the highway, which, let me tell you, I am thoroughly sick of doing."

"Did you see the game?" asked George, sliding into place beside his father in the front of the car.

Chuck opened the back door and hopped inside, pushing his knapsack to the floor. He was anxious to hear the doctor's reply.

"Sure, I saw it. Where were you, George?"

"What do you mean, Dad?"

"I mean, where *were* you? You and Chuck came into play at the end of the game. The rest of the time, nobody could find you, and the coach was going nuts. That's why the team lost today to Buffalo. You guys are out of the state finals because of this, and I'll tell you, son, the principal may be asking you these same questions tomorrow."

Oh-oh. Chuck and George were in trouble. They could get kicked off the team, or maybe even kicked out of school, because of this Labyrinth of Doom mess. Chuck tried to think of answers that might make sense to people:

We were late to the game because my ankle got twisted on the highway.

We were late to the game because my cat was tangled in some vines in the ditch.

We were late to the game because our watches stopped.

Oh, brother. Everything Chuck thought of sounded so lame. He asked, "Doctor Croute, what day is it? And what's the time?"

George peered out the window, refusing to look at his father or respond to his father's puzzled stare. "Well, boys, it's Saturday at 10 PM, if that helps you. Now, where have you been all afternoon?"

"Where's Digger McGraw?" asked Chuck, and George shot him a look that said, *Why on earth do you want to know where that creep is?*

Doctor Croute steered the car down the snow-lined street in front of the school and turned right onto the main road leading to the highway. There were no smiley-face boulders anywhere, no sliding-door contraptions, no gigantic granite or ice walls. Just village cottages and Victorian mansions, just garbage bins set out for the trashman on Monday, just lights twinkling in the windows and those fake candles glowing in the windows of the bigger homes. No winds, no storms. It was a peaceful evening. Chuck wondered if his mother was waiting for him at home.

"So where is Digger?" Chuck repeated. And then he added, "And did they ever fix that uh . . . blockade . . . down in the city?"

The car moved left and onto the highway, sweeping past Candy Malone's house and the swamps on either side of the road.

Doctor Croute said, "How would I know where Digger McGraw is? I don't know. The last I remember, the coach tossed Digger McGraw and Jack Fastolf off the hockey team after they beat you up, Chuck, on the ice. It doesn't matter. I want to know where the two of you have been all night. Oh, and about that 'blockade'? I don't know what you're talking about." The doctor sighed and started grumbling. Chuck figured it would be smart to remain quiet and not ask any further questions.

The car turned into Chuck's driveway. Schnooky was on the front windowsill. Chuck's mother peered from the window, and then the front door opened. *Chuck was home.* Most important, his mother was home and safe.

"You have a pretty cool mother," said George.

An odd comment. "Well, thanks," said Chuck.

Then George said to his father, "Chuck has a nice mother."

"Yes, I know, son. George, you've never been in trouble before. What's happening? Please tell me."

"I never knew Mom. I mean, you've been a great dad and everything, but I don't know—today, something just came over me. I started thinking about Mom a lot. I started missing her, as if I'd seen her and known her, even briefly, before she disappeared."

"That was a long time ago," said Doctor Croute. His eyes softened, and his smile was now warm, not cold, and he was no longer grumbling. "You were trying to remember your mother today, son?"

"Sort of," said George. "I was with Chuck, that much I know." He looked at Chuck, as if asking Chuck to help him with the explanation.

Chuck lifted his backpack from the floor, put his hand on the latch that would open the car door. His own mother was waiting for him, and he really wanted to see her, now more than ever before. He'd almost lost her to the Labyrinth of Doom, much as George had lost Mary Croute many years before in another, much older Labyrinth of Doom, one created from a shift of energy beneath the earth at Chartres Cathedral in France. Perhaps the Demon had almost come to earth and reality back then, too, and the shift in energies had oozed negative forces into the Chartres labyrinth, scooping Mary Croute into another domain and reality.

Chuck said, "I was telling George about my mother, Doctor Croute, how weird I sometimes think it is that George has only you, yet I have only my mother. See, it's like opposites."

George nodded. "Yes, go on."

Chuck really didn't want to continue this weird explanation. He didn't know what to say. Obviously, Doctor Croute didn't remember talking to Chuck about labyrinth software, about Chartres, or about his wife. Doctor Croute treated Chuck as if he were just another kid, not someone special who had entered a Labyrinth of Doom and closed it down forever.

Suddenly, Chuck wanted to know: "Has anyone trespassed, sir, into your house lately, and maybe taken some of your software?"

Doctor Croute glared at him. "No, son. Why do you ask?"

"Your labyrinth algorithm software, perhaps?"

"No, Chuck, nothing of the kind has happened."

So time had shifted somehow, made everything sane again, yet pushed George and Chuck into the state semifinal hockey game while simultaneously pushing time for Digger to a point preceding the bully's theft of Doctor Croute's software. Chuck couldn't understand or puzzle through the time implications.

Of course, he figured, if time gets screwed up at all, who's to say how it gets screwed up or how it gets fixed again? Perhaps this is just another mystery of life, as is the Demon himself and the Demon's world. If indeed the Demon's penetration into reality could cause this much trouble on earth, what would happen if the Demon got lost elsewhere in the universe? *The results would be an absolute Cosmic Storm!*

"Well," said Chuck, opening the car door and sliding outside—he was ready to terminate this bizarre conversation and go inside to Schnooky and his mother—"I hope you and the coach and principal and all can forgive us, Doctor Croute. George got really sad today, thinking about his mother. I'm his best friend, you see. I thought it was more important to hang out with George than be at this game. We got a little lost, walking around the village, that's all. We lost track of time."

Pretty lame, and it bordered on a lie without being a lie. As a rule, Chuck didn't lie. And, besides, they *had* been worried about Mary Croute, they *had* lost track of time, they *had* gotten totally lost in the Labyrinth of Doom, starting with the sliding-door maze in the village, not to mention the maze of Schnooky's head in the school. Yeah, Chuck had told the truth. "I gotta go now," he said, "but if you guys wanna talk later, call me. I mean that."

George nodded and smiled. Doctor Croute also nodded and smiled. Everything would be okay. Doctor Croute would convince Coach Flanders and Mr. Calhoun that George and Chuck had missed the game for a good reason. Well, if not a good reason, at least for a reason that wouldn't get the boys kicked off the team or out of school. Everybody knew that times had changed since the 1950s, when kids and families were all vanilla-like. Nowadays, Chuck's physician drilled him for an hour prior to physicals about his emotional state of mind:

Do you miss your father?
Are there guns in your house?
Do you like schoolwork?

Do you know that rusty used needles found in the gutter can give you AIDS?

Chuck barely understood most of the doctor's questions, and his mother found the questions to be an invasion of her privacy, and of Chuck's privacy. She also considered the questions to be disrespectful to her as a decent, hardworking single mother. It all made Chuck very mad.

So in today's world, an excuse such as *George was sad, missing his dead mother* was no big deal. The worst it could do was push Chuck and George into an hour-long session with the school counselor, who would smile insincerely while thinking of her comfy home and her own perfect children.

Oh, brother. Chuck hated those scenes—they made him angrier than anything else on earth. But it still beat getting thrown off the team.

The counselor would ask Chuck and George more dumb questions, such as:

How does it feel to know your mother's dead?

How does it feel to know your father hates your mother?

Do you get enough food to eat?

Do you have any hobbies?

Do you know the proper procedures for handling loaded guns?

Chuck's real answer to it all?

There are disrupting forces in life that we may never fully comprehend, such as why everything's formed in a labyrinth configuration; why my father wanted my youth instead of letting me have it; why negative energies burst forth and consume our positive energies; why the serene, curving paths of harmony suddenly twist into hard, lonely edges.

I'll tell you the answer, guys: if you're patient enough, you can come out of the prickly negative points of life, the hard edges, back onto the serene, curving path. You just have to be patient and keep working at it, and everything will be okay. Stay steady. Don't let the bad forces pull you down.

Inside Chuck's house, the walls were light green, and the rug was forest green. The fake-wood banister was warm brown. The ancient cat meowed her hello and rubbed against Chuck's legs. The lamp pole cast warmth across the worn old living room, and there against the wall, across from the flowered pink-and-green sofa, were Chuck's video-game console and the television. Chuck was one lucky guy.

And he was home again, safe with his mother and Schnooky in The Dump with the laundromat water on the highway one mile outside of town.

"What's for dinner?" he asked.

Your Quest Journal:

1. Save the hockey team from Digger McGraw: SUCCESS.
2. Find the secret of the tardigrades: SUCCESS.
3. Go to the Ice Cap: SUCCESS.
4. Find the Labyrinth of Doom: SUCCESS.
5. Teach Melody some video-game basics: SUCCESS.
6. Learn how to control time: SUCCESS.
7. Unlock the tenth level: SUCCESS.

8. Get an escort to Greenland: SUCCESS.
9. Find the center of the Schnooky maze: SUCCESS.
10. Solve the Einstein's head maze: SUCCESS.
11. Learn how to program complex mathematical mazes on the computer: SUCCESS.
12. Solve the sliding-door maze to get out of the village: SUCCESS.
13. Find Mary Croute: SUCCESS.
14. Fence Digger with a dowsing rod and win: SUCCESS.
15. Force Jack Fastolf to stop selling beer to little kids: UNKNOWN RESULTS.
16. Wrestle Digger McGraw and beat him with the Batman technique: SUCCESS.
17. Find the Genesa Crystal, a.k.a. the peacock jewel: SUCCESS.
18. Find the secret of the red shoes: SUCCESS.
19. Beat all the games to get the superhero powers: SUCCESS.
20. Find the basement of the Tower of Darkness: SUCCESS.
21. Pick the lock to the castle: SUCCESS.
22. Meet your fears and conquer them: SUCCESS.
23. Survive a meeting with Mom and Dad: SUCCESS.
24. Survive once again: SUCCESS.

Your Inventory:

- Hockey stick
- Photos of hockey heroes
- Memory of the Tower of Darkness world
- Photo of Scott Metcalfe and the Demon of Runes
- Egyptian painting

- Candle in a wall holder
- Ankh
- Screws
- Most Manic award
- Fists of Fury award
- One club
- One wad of dynamite
- *Greenland's Underground Delights*, the textbook
- One broken wok
- Construction worker's hard hat with lamp
- Disk of Doctor Croute's software
- One dowsing rod
- Bright pink jump rope
- Red snowboard

NHL 2001: GAME OVER. NEW GAME?

SSX SNOWBOARDING: GAME OVER. NEW GAME?

SUMMONER: GAME OVER. NEW GAME?

TIMESPLITTERS: GAME OVER. NEW GAME?

THE BOUNCER: GAME OVER. NEW GAME?